Twice the Trouble

by

Sandra Dailey

Twice the Trouble

Cover Art by *Debbie Taylor*

The Wild Rose Press, Inc.
PO Box 708
Adams Basin, NY 14410-0708
Visit us at www.thewildrosepress.com

Publishing History
First Champagne Rose Edition, 2013
Digital ISBN 978-1-61217-798-4
Print ISBN 978-1-62830-098-7

Published in the United States of America

Lacey let her legs dangle over the end of the dock. The pink twilight sky made the surface of the lake look like a sheet of lavender tinted glass. If she had to leave the Double J, the lake was what she'd miss most. She'd never lived in a place where she couldn't see the water from her window. But she'd decided that if she did have to move, it would be to a new town. She'd make a fresh start. She'd go to a place where people didn't know every detail of her past. Her kids shouldn't have to hear gossip about her.

Jerrod was clearly ashamed of her. That had been the worst pain she'd ever experienced. Then, to solidify his low opinion of her, she'd struck him. She wished she'd never gotten out of bed that morning.

Alex's footsteps sounded on the wooden planks' but she didn't turn around. She was too embarrassed. He sat on the corner of the dock with his back against the rail post, facing her right side.

"If you're thinking of jumping in the lake to end it all, let me know in advance." He stretched out his legs and crossed his ankles. "These shoes set me back a couple hundred bucks. I'd want a chance to take them off before I dive in after you. There's also my wallet and cell phone to consider."

Alex always could make her smile.

"I've never heard Superman complain about having his cape dry-cleaned," she replied. "I've never seen Batman ask for time to remove his utility belt. The Incredible Hulk never asks for a safety pin. If you're going to be a hero, you've got to be tough."

Alex's eyes widened. "So that's who you've been dating since I've been gone."

Praise for *THE CHIEF'S PROPOSAL*

"I quite liked these two [characters], with their differing goals and motivations, along with a load of conflicts that they need each other to resolve. There are also a few deliciously bad villains. Dailey is a good writer, and her characterizations are excellent. *THE CHIEF'S PROPOSAL* is a very nice love story with a few twists that you will surely enjoy."

~Alberta, Manic Readers Review
~*~

"Who would have known that an eagle and a dove would make a perfect match? *THE CHIEF'S PROPOSAL* is well written and it flows well. Believe me that 204 pages went by so quickly that when I got to the epilogue, it felt that I had just started reading the book. I highly recommend this romantic and giddy story with a great plot for anyone in need of a quick romantic read."

~Cozyreader, The Romantic Reviews
~*~

THE CHIEF'S PROPOSAL
is available from The Wild Rose Press, Inc.

Dedication

I dedicate this book to my husband Lee.
Without his love, support, inspiration, patience,
housekeeping, cooking, and comedy relief,
it would never have been written.

Chapter One

"Mr. Benson, a young lady just arrived. She says she needs to speak to you urgently."

Damn, just when it looked like he might finally get home early on a Friday afternoon. Visions of a cold bottle of beer and a juicy steak had been teasing him all day.

Alex held down the intercom button. "I don't see any appointments on my calendar, Mary Ann. Did she say what this is about?"

"No sir," Mary Ann answered over the intercom. "But she seems really desperate. I've got a feeling about her."

If there was one thing Alex had learned not to ignore, it was Mary Ann's instincts. Sometimes he thought she must be clairvoyant. That's how she'd moved into the position as his personal assistant so quickly. She could read people at a glance.

"Well, okay then." He picked up his pen and opened his schedule book. "What's the lady's name?"

"It's Ms. Carlyle," Mary Ann replied.

"Pardon me, could you repeat that?" His heart thumped double-time in his tight chest.

"I said Carlyle sir, Ms. Carlyle. Do you want me to get more information?"

"No, that's all right. Send her in."

Alex turned his leather chair around to face the

Orlando skyline. It wasn't the rooftops that he saw in the glaring afternoon sun, but the small lake in his memory. He recalled the sparkling beads of water that splashed around Lacey Carlyle's feet as she swung them off the end of the pier. Her long copper hair flashed like flames around her shoulders. A light sprinkling of freckles covered her straight delicate nose. Her eyes were the color of robin eggs and her soft coral lips invited long, deep kisses.

He cursed the mention of the name Carlyle, but he would have thought about Lacey before the day was over in any case. He thought about her every day. He thought about the way she'd made him feel as though he could fly without wings. Then he'd remember the way her betrayal had felt, as if he'd crashed to the ground, broken and bleeding. He'd been such an idiot to get involved with her, immature and naive.

What would he do if Lacey Carlyle were to walk through his door one day? He'd show her he wasn't a young, tenderhearted boy anymore. He was in control of his life. Hell, he was in control of his world. He'd make her stand accountable for the way she'd destroyed his dreams.

Alex rubbed his right hand up and down the long, left sleeve of his starched, white dress shirt. It was a habit he had now whenever he became agitated. Damn Lacey Carlyle.

****

It had taken Lacey a week to track down the address for East Coast Land Development's corporate office. By sheer luck, it was only a couple of hours from her home. Now, she stood outside the solid oak door of the president and CEO. She stared at the brass nameplate at the side of the door. A. J. Benson. This had to be a bad omen. Never mind that she'd driven two hours to find him, if she weren't so desperate, she'd turn around and leave.

The name Benson was common, but always succeeded in bringing back memories of his broken promises and the pain of her broken heart. It had been thirteen years since she'd seen Alex, but the pain was still fresh. She took a deep breath. This was no time for a trip down memory lane. Lacey gathered her courage and knocked on the door.

A deep masculine voice came from inside. "Come in."

Lacey stepped into the large office and was awed by the floor to ceiling windows that looked out over the city. The only things obstructing her view was a wide mahogany desk and the back of a tall, brown leather chair. The chair turned slowly to face her.

Gazing into familiar, jade green eyes, Lacey's throat and chest tightened painfully. Three thoughts occurred to her simultaneously. One, she had never loved any man more than this one. A thrill ran down her spine at the sight of him. Two, no one had ever hurt her the way he had. A chill ran up the nape of her neck. And three, this couldn't be happening. Could he possibly be the one responsible for the disaster her life had become? Why wouldn't he be? He'd upended her life once before.

Suddenly the sensation of spinning overtook her and there wasn't anything within her reach to grab hold of. The moment her legs collapsed, his hands tightened around her upper arms and guided her onto a nearby sofa. How had he reached her so quickly? Had time stood still for that moment?

Neither of them spoke right away. Lacey couldn't pull her eyes from him. It was like seeing a ghost. But he wasn't a ghost. He was a demon from her past.

She took note of how he had changed. His jaw was harder under a neatly trimmed beard. His neck was thicker and blended into wide, strong shoulders. The long, lanky body he'd had as a teen had matured into a fuller, more muscular build. He'd traded his T-shirts and blue jeans for a crisp white dress shirt, silk tie, and charcoal slacks. His chestnut curls had been clipped into a short, professional style. But his eyes were the same. She'd never forget his eyes. She couldn't. Was this some kind of cruel joke her mind was playing?

"What are you doing here, Lacey?"

No hello? No how are you? No are you all right after nearly fainting in the middle of my office? Lacey took immediate offence at the question, delivered with a stern expression. Who was he, to speak to her that way after what she'd been through? Still, it took another moment for her to gather her thoughts. She'd almost forgotten why she was there.

"I need to speak to you about the property you purchased." It was a struggle to regain her composure.

Alex walked to a small bar in the corner and opened a refrigerator that was concealed there. He removed two bottles of water. "I own property all the way up the eastern seaboard. That's what I do. I buy land, develop it, and sell it for a profit. I'm not intimately familiar with every parcel."

"You know exactly what property I'm talking about, Alex, the property in Indian Lakes-my property."

One at a time, Alex twisted the caps off the bottles

and placed them on the bar. "I beg to disagree, Lacey. If I bought the land, it belongs to me. It doesn't even touch your grandfather's place. I made sure of that."

So, he hadn't completely forgotten her. Lacey's spine straightened and her chin tilted up. "I don't live with my grandfather. I've leased that land on the east shore for eight years. I was supposed to have first chance at it, when it came up for sale. I didn't have the funding together before you snatched it up."

Lacey watched his eyes scan down her worn blouse and old denim skirt. She was painfully aware of how outdated, worn out and cheap they were. They may have been bought at the Goodwill store, but it had been so long ago, she couldn't remember. The way his brow cocked arrogantly made her want to slap his face.

"Do you have the funding now, Lacey?"

She looked back at the windows to avoid Alex's gaze. "Not quite, but I'm working on it."

Alex slid into a chair to her left and passed her one of the water bottles. "I was told there was an old farmhouse on that land, but I wasn't aware it was being rented out."

Lacey heard the annoyance in his voice and believed him. "The plan is to divide the place into two-acre lots. Ranchettes are popular now. It would be more affordable for you to just buy the lot you're currently living on. Maybe I could even get you a good deal for...old-time's sake."

Panic rose in Lacey's stomach like a battalion of butterflies. "It's not just an old house, it's my home! I have twenty head of cattle, two-dozen pigs, three horses, and two border collies. I can't keep all of them on two acres. My vegetable garden is larger than that. I need the whole place! It's how I make a living!" Lacey stood and started to pace the floor in front of the desk. "All I need is a little time. Given another month or so, I know I can put together the money to pay what you gave for it."

"I've already made you my best offer, Lacey," Alex countered. "This is business, nothing personal about it. I already have interested investors. I don't make money by waiting for maybes."

"You sure as hell didn't mind keeping me waiting," Lacey blurted. "I waited for you for such a long time before I had to move on. Now you're turning my life upside down again. What did I do to make you hate me this much? Not a word from you in thirteen years. Now I stand to lose everything, because of you. Why are you doing this to me, Alex?"

Alex's jaws hardened and his face turned an angry shade of red. "How can you say that? I wrote to you two, sometimes three times a week. I didn't quit writing until my letters started coming back unopened. You're the one that walked away, not me."

"That's a lie," Lacey retorted.

Neither of them realized that they were shouting until Mary Ann tapped on the door and cracked it open to look inside. "Is everything all right in here?" she asked.

"Yes, everything is fine," Alex said in a calm voice. "I think I'll knock off early today. Why don't you go on home? Have a nice weekend with your family."

The woman nervously chewed her bottom lip as she looked back and forth between them.

"I'll see Ms. Carlyle out as I leave," Alex assured

her.

After she'd closed the door, Alex removed the jacket of his suit from a coat rack by the door. He slid his left arm into the sleeve, but when he pulled the jacket around to push his right arm through, the left sleeve drew back to reveal the scars covering his wrist and the back of his hand.

Lacey gasped. She was embarrassed by her reaction and quickly tried to explain. "Several months after you left, I heard you'd been hurt in an accident. By that time, your parents had moved away and I couldn't find out what had happened. I didn't even know if you were still alive."

Alex straightened his jacket and tugged his sleeve back in place. "What does it matter now? If you had wanted to be in touch with me, if you truly hadn't received my letters, you still could have gotten my address from my parents. They stayed on Indian Lakes for the first few months after I left."

"I couldn't talk to your parents. They felt I was to blame for you giving up your plans for college and going into the Navy. As more time went by without word from you, I figured you regretted that decision and blamed me too. It might surprise you to know that I've also made sacrifices."

"Yeah, yeah," Alex sneered. "We both made sacrifices. You gave up your virginity and I gave up my freedom for a few years because of it. Sounds fair to me."

"You did what you wanted to do. I didn't want you to go. If you'll recall, I begged you to stay."

Alex grabbed his car keys and wallet from his desk drawer and slammed it shut. "And then you didn't want me to come back. Isn't that why I never heard from you?"

"Don't expect me to feel sorry for you." Lacey spread her arms and turned in a circle to indicate the entire room, maybe the entire world. "You have it all, Alex. What more could you possibly want?"

Alex's face turned to cold stone. He was silent for several seconds. "I need to get out of here," he finally said. "Take a ride with me."

"Why should I go anywhere with you?" Lacey asked.

"The more important questions are, how badly do you want that land, and what are you willing to do to keep it?"

Chapter Two

The heat radiated off the asphalt in waves and, even though the inside of his BMW was air conditioned, the blood in Alex's veins simmered. His body acted like a divining rod to Lacey still. He needed to get himself under control.

How dare she accuse him of leaving her behind? She had no idea how desperately he'd wanted her, needed her, during the worst, most lonely, and painful time of his life.

So, she thought he had it all, couldn't want more. Well, he could want a hell of a lot more. He was a man who took what he wanted without apology. She'd soon find that out. He might be making the biggest mistake of his life, but she'd be the one to suffer this time. He'd tie her down, and then walk away, just the way she'd accused him. This time their parting would be on his terms.

He didn't have the need for a woman like he had as a boy, but he knew how to make a woman want him. He'd fill her with desire in every way possible. Then he'd walk. That's all he would need to put the memory of her behind him once and for all.

He'd resisted glancing at Lacey for as long as he could. She had barely changed over the last thirteen years. Her hair had been cut into a soft angle that didn't quite touch her shoulders, but it was still the color of a bright, new penny. Her makeup was light and natural. The freckles on her nose were still evident. Her eyes were the same clear, aqua blue. And her soft lips were the thing fantasies were made from.

How many men had acted out their fantasies with her? It shouldn't matter; he'd had other women but it did, and the thought made his blood hit the boiling point. If he didn't distract himself, he'd wreck his car.

"I noticed you still use your maiden name. Didn't you ever get married?"

The sudden question seemed to startle Lacey and she blinked a few times. "Some women keep their maiden names and some take them back after a divorce."

Evasive, he should have expected as much. A sneer touched the corner of his lips. "So, which are you, Lacey, the modern bride or the bitter divorcée?"

"Neither," she admitted.

"You've never married then?"

"I could have. I simply chose not to."

"I'm not surprised. Was I the first on a list of discarded lovers?" Was that a look of regret on her pretty face? Surely not. She'd made her choice.

After a moment of silence, Lacey returned his question, "What about you, Alex? Is there a Mrs. Benson somewhere, past or present?"

"Nope, never married," Alex replied. "Women tell me I have trust issues. Can you imagine that?"

Alex was still curious. "Is there anyone special in your life now, a fiancé, a boyfriend, a girlfriend?"

Lacey glared at him. "My work doesn't give me much time for a social life."

"Yeah, I know what you mean. I usually work from

sunup to sundown and I travel a lot. My so-called relationships have a short shelf life." Why had he admitted that? He turned into a parking lot and slipped into a spot near a large, brick building.

"I hope your business won't take long here. I want to be home before dark."

Exiting the cool car, they met a wall of stifling heat. "It shouldn't take long." Alex walked to her side of the car and took her arm. He'd decided what trap would have the most impact. "You have identification with you, I hope."

Lacey's gaze snapped to the Orange County Courthouse sign. Her eyes widened. "Are you planning to have me evicted from my house? If so, you're in the wrong county. And no matter where you go, you'll be in for one hell of a fight."

"What do I look like, Lacey, some kind of villain? I promise I won't tie you to any railroad tracks. We're simply here to apply for our marriage license."

"Our what? You've got to be kidding!" Lacey tried to pull her arm away, but his grip tightened. "I wouldn't marry you now if hounds from hell were nipping at my heels."

"Maybe you won't have to." Alex reasoned. "If you can come up with the money for the property by the end of a month, you're off the hook. If not, you'll have to be my wife to keep the place."

"That's all you're giving me? One month, thirty lousy days?" She tried to pull away from him and failed again. "You know I won't be able to get that kind of money in that short time. This is extortion, plain and simple. You are a villain, you asshole!"

"Maybe you're right. Those railroad tracks are

sounding pretty damn good right now." Alex couldn't hold back a grin. "You know, you're really kind of cute when you curse. I think that's the first time I've ever heard you do it."

Alex started tugging her toward the courthouse steps, but Lacey dug in her heels and made the task twice as hard.

"You know this won't work," she said. "We don't even know each other anymore. Why are you doing this to me?"

Alex stopped and glared down at her. "There was a time when this was all either of us wanted. Do you find the idea of being my wife that repulsive now, Lacey?"

Lacey straightened and pushed her hair out of her face. "You don't understand. I have a lot of responsibilities. More than you can imagine. I couldn't be a good wife for anyone. Dammit, I wouldn't even know how to be married."

The sincere sound in her voice and the pleading look in her eyes made Alex soften slightly. "Does anyone start out knowing how to be married? I don't think so. They stumble through it together and figure it out."

"You're talking about people who love each other, Alex. That's not us, not anymore."

She looked so sad, it softened him up a little more. It had been a shock, seeing her today, touching her, hearing her voice. This plan wasn't only about punishing her for the past. He needed time to sort through the myriad of emotions bombarding him. In the meantime, he couldn't let her slip through his fingers.

"Here's the deal. We'll only see each other on occasional weekends. You'll live on Indian Lakes and

I'll stay here. Can you handle that in exchange for your precious home? A very large and somewhat expensive piece of property, I might add. It would just be a part-time marriage, but a marriage none the less. I'd expect you to be loyal to me, only me. That's the deal if you want to keep your home sweet home."

Lacey gave a frustrated sigh. "How long would you expect this arrangement to last?"

Shit, was she already planning the divorce? It seemed she couldn't get away from him fast enough. His heart hardened right back to the way it had started. "We'll spend time together until I get bored, which probably won't take long, but I won't allow a divorce for thirteen years. I figure that's how much time you owe me."

"I don't owe you a single second," Lacey retorted.

"Do you want the property or not?"

If Lacey ground her teeth any harder, she'd crack a molar. "The property would belong to me, free and clear, I'd hold the deed to the entire place?"

"You'd still have to pay the property tax and insurance every year, but yeah. I can have a prenuptial agreement drawn up first thing Monday morning."

Lacey looked around and then shook her head. "I don't know how I'd manage to come here on weekends. My grandfather is watching the place now, but he's not as strong as he used to be. Besides that, my truck is on its last legs."

"You'd only need to be here if I have any kind of social engagement, otherwise, I can come to Indian Lakes. It'd be nice to get away from the city once in a while."

"Where would you stay in Indian Lakes?"

Alex released her. He stepped back and crossed his arms. "With my wife, of course. You've got ten seconds to decide if that's going to be you. If not, you'd better go home and start packing."

Lacey made another deep sigh. "Let's get this over with then."

Alex followed his blushing bride up the stone steps.

At the clerk's desk, they were given family law booklets to read, how romantic. Then, they were directed to the waiting area.

Alex sat on hard plastic chair against the wall. Lacey chose a chair three seats away.

A young woman sitting catty-cornered from Lacey leaned forward to get her attention. "This has got to be the most exciting day of my life," she said breathlessly. "My fiancé and I took the premarital prep course so we could get married right away. Is that what the two of you did?"

"No." Lacey smiled. "I didn't expect to be here at all, but my ex-boyfriend is blackmailing me, so here I am."

Alex listened, but didn't look up from his booklet. "Lacey, behave," he said in a bored tone. "Just because you don't like something doesn't mean you have to spoil it for everyone."

The young woman looked confused and a little alarmed, but she quickly recovered when a clerk called her name.

After forty long minutes, it was Alex and Lacey's turn to stand at the glass-partitioned counter. A middle-aged woman with half glasses, a pencil in her hair, and a jaded expression pushed a form through a slot under the glass. "Fill this out and return it with both of your picture IDs, please."

Alex was amused by the way Lacey blocked his view while she filled out her half of the form. He made a point of reading every word she'd written before completing his half. The questions were generic and nothing he didn't already know about her.

"Did the two of you take the premarital preparation course within the last thirty days?" the clerk asked.

"No," Alex answered. "We just ran into each other this afternoon."

The clerk rolled her eyes, as though she'd heard that line a hundred times before. "It'll cost ninety-three-fifty, and then you'll have a three-day waiting period."

"Do you really think that's long enough?" Lacey said. "This is a big step, and I could use a few more months to think about it."

"I hear that U-Haul has great local rates." Alex peeled a hundred dollar bill from his money clip and slid it through the window slot. He turned to Lacey. "You can keep the change. Apply it toward your moving expenses."

The ride back to his office building was silent as before, but somehow seemed more so. It wasn't because he didn't know what to say. There just didn't seem to be anything left to say.

Alex parked in the same choice spot he'd left earlier and shut off the ignition. He walked around to the passenger side and opened Lacey's door.

"Why are you doing this to me?" she asked again.

"Isn't it obvious?" Alex smirked. "Retribution."

Alex cringed when Lacey slammed the door of his treasured BMW and strode to the next island in the lot.

She stopped beside an older than dirt Ford pickup with more primer than paint and rust holes along the bottom the size of baseballs.

Alex rushed to catch up to her. "You can't be serious," He looked the truck over.

"Hey, this happens to be an antique." Lacey seemed truly offended. "It just needs a little fixing up. I admit it's not pretty, but what do you expect from a farm truck?"

"I expect you to be able to make it home without having to add three quarts of oil."

"Seriously, Alex, I'll be fine. I've been driving this thing forever."

"You, and how many others before you?" Alex pulled a business card from his breast pocket. "Call me when you get home. Just so I know that *Old Rusty* got you there safely."

Lacey snatched the card from his fingers. "Whatever, I really need to get on the road. Granddad is going to be furious that I'm so late." She turned and opened the creaky driver's door.

"What, no kiss good-bye?"

"Now you're the one who's not serious." Alex spun her around and trapped her against the side of the truck bed. Impulsively, he took her mouth in a deep, bone-melting kiss. He didn't know why he did it, but he realized that he'd wanted to, since the moment he saw her standing in his office. It was still a natural, primal instinct to press his body to hers and find a way inside. As much as he hated her, his body still craved her. From the desperate little whine she emitted as she leaned close, he suspected Lacey's body might still remember his as well.

His hands roamed down her narrow back and pressed her closer. Her smell, her taste, her warmth…were even better than he remembered. He tried to relieve the throbbing tension in his groin by rubbing against her soft belly.

The feel of his hard length must have brought Lacey to her senses. She pulled away touching her fingers to her lips and looking stunned. "We can't do this. I'm not ready for this."

He'd been foolish to go so far, but Alex was an expert at covering his thoughts and feelings. He grinned and winked before he walked away. "Gotcha."

Chapter Three

"What took you so damned long to get back? It's nearly dark outside."

Clarence Carlyle slowly lifted himself out of the rocking chair in Lacey's living room. He looked older every day with thin, gray hair, and dull, lifeless eyes. His hands were covered with liver spots and the veins stood out on them. His lined face held a permanent scowl. How long had it been since the man felt the urge to smile?

"You're welcome to have supper here tonight, Granddad."

"You know I don't see well enough to drive at night," he roared. "I suppose, if I ran off into a ditch and died, it wouldn't be any skin off your nose."

Lacey was never sure how to respond when he said things like that. She wondered if her grandfather had any love for her at all. She'd been nothing but a burden and a disappointment to him since her parents died. It was a fact he'd never hidden.

"At least tell me that your trip wasn't wasted," he groused.

"I spoke to the man who owns the real estate company. He wants to divide this place into two-acre lots and sell it off as ranchettes, but he's agreed to give me a month to come up with the money to buy the whole place."

"It's too bad you don't have the money. This'll be a miserable town if a bunch of city dudes move in trying to act like ranchers."

"Are you sure you can't help me out, Granddad? I'd be guaranteed a loan with your signature." Lacey hated to beg. Especially when she knew the outcome would be unsuccessful.

Clarence Carlyle had been the president of Indian Lakes' only bank for forty years. Everyone knew and respected him. Even though he was an unpleasant sort, you never knew when you might have to make a late payment or need a loan. He still carried a lot of clout in the community.

"You moved out of my house eight years ago," he said. "I told you then that this farm was a bad idea. You're trying to do the work of a man. Nothing good can come from it. Now, maybe you can get a regular job and start acting like a woman. You're lucky enough the man was willing to talk to you. Why he'd bother, I can't imagine. Surely he could see that you're not up for this responsibility."

Lacey's face flamed with temper. "I've run this farm for eight years. It's kept food on the table and a roof overhead."

Clarence sauntered to the door with a limp. "You're going to have to figure this out on your own, girl. I'm too old to keep pulling you out of messes."

He didn't know how badly those words hurt her. He probably wouldn't care if he did.

"The man's looking for a wife," Lacey informed him. "He says if I marry him, he'll let me keep the place."

Clarence croaked out a dry laugh. "Are you that

stupid? He'll spend a night or two with you, and then be on his way. He'll leave you out on the street. No self-respecting man would have anything more than that to do with you."

"What if the man was Alex Benson?" Lacey countered.

Clarence stopped in the doorway. He looked more furious than Lacey had ever seen him. "After all I've done for you. I can't believe that you'd speak that man's name in my presence."

Lacey jumped when the screen door slammed behind him. He had a way of making her feel small and dirty. Sometimes she wished he'd let her be taken into foster care after her parents died. Her life would have been so much different now.

The fatal car accident was the most horrible event of her life, but seventeen-year-old Lacey had taken a small amount of comfort in the fact that her parents died together. They'd been so in love, neither of them would have survived without the other. Sometimes she wished she'd been with them.

On the evening after the funeral, everyone in town gathered at her grandfather's house. They all loved John and Lily Carlyle.

"What a sweet couple," they all said. "It's such a shame."

Of course there's always a fly in the ointment. Miss Dell, from the drugstore cosmetics counter, had pulled Lacey aside. "Lacey, honey, you're a lucky girl. Your grandfather can raise you like a proper lady now. I don't know what your parents were thinking when they let you work in the fields like a common farmhand."

Lacey had been brought up to respect her elders. She made no reply to Miss Dell's callous comment. She walked out her grandfather's back door and then broke into a run for the lake. That's where Alex had found her. She and Alex had known each other all their lives, but that was the first time he'd seen her as a woman.

"Mom, are you okay?"

Lacey was startled from her memories. She smiled down at her son and brushed the unruly curls from his forehead. "Yeah, I'm okay. I was just having a moment of nostalgia. Old people tend to do that, you know. Did you get your chores done like I asked you to?"

"Yes ma'am, for the most part." Jerrod dug his toe into the dirt and twisted out a divot. "That's what I wanted to talk to you about."

Lacey raised a brow. She knew the bull was about to leave the barn. "Oh?"

"Well, yes'm. You see, Granddad says inside chores are a woman's work and I tend to agree."

Lacey rolled her eyes. Clarence Carlyle had struck again. She forced herself to look sincere. "I've always thought that was an old-fashioned notion, but if that's what you really think, we could give it a try."

Jerrod's smile beamed in the moonlight. "Really Mom, do you mean it? No more dishes or dusting and stuff?"

"Sure," Lacey shrugged. "I'll miss working with you, but I think you can take care of this place on your own now. The new fence posts and wire are in the barn for the west side of the pasture. You'll find the paint in there too. After you lay the new floor on the porch, you'll need to paint the railing, and then the shutters will have to be done to match. Maybe you should clean out the feed bins first though. You can do that along with mucking out the stalls. If you get a chance to take a break, the dogs need to be bathed and dipped. I want to start you out easy."

Jerrod nearly shook with panic. "I'd have to do all that by myself?"

"Well son." Lacey smiled. "You are the only man around here and all that stuff is man's work, according to your granddad. I guess I'll finally have enough time to teach your sister how to knit and sew. Personally, I'm not looking forward to her cooking, but if you can take it, I guess I can too. She has to learn woman's work sooner or later."

"Not even Granddad can take Jenna's cooking, and he'll eat about anything." Jerrod grimaced. "I'm thinking he may be wrong about this man's work and woman's work stuff. Things get done pretty well around here the way they are."

"I've always thought we made a good team." Lacey kissed the top of Jerrod's head and watched him walk back to the house.

She looked across the lake and waited for her grandfather's kitchen light to come on before she followed. She did care about the old man, no matter how mean he was. He had taken care of her all those years ago and, besides the kids, he was all the family she had.

****

Seaman Apprentice Alex Benson walked out of the mailroom with two envelopes in his hand. He'd been disappointed so many times, he was afraid to look at them.

He'd been in the Navy for six months. The first

two were spent on basic training, the second two, training for a job as a carrier crewmember. Now that he was aboard ship, his routine was still hectic. No matter how busy he was, though, he still found time to write to Lacey. He wished he could say the same for her. Not once had she answered one of his letters.

Lacey had been upset with him for going into the Navy. Why couldn't she understand that he was trying to prepare for their future? College would have been expensive and taken too much time. With the Navy, he'd be trained in a career field within a year and he was already putting away money.

Aboard ship, he was more homesick for Lacey than he'd been on dry land. Her continued silence caused him to suspect all kinds of crazy things. Could she have lied when she said she loved him? Had she gotten tired of waiting for him already? Could she be seeing someone else?

Alex gathered his courage and turned over the first envelope in his hand. It had Lacey's address scrolled across the front in his own handwriting, and over it were large letters written in red marker, RETURN TO SENDER. It was the third letter to be returned unopened.

The second envelope contained a Christmas card from his parents. "Merry friggin' Christmas to me," Alex muttered as he passed the engine room door.

A sound like thunder resonated through the narrow passage. Alex turned in time to see a ball of fire shoot toward him from inside the room. It threw him against the wall. The empty corridor was suddenly filled with the sounds of running footsteps and shouting. Smoke filled his lungs. A screaming siren was accompanied by a pulsing red light. Then there was nothing but unimaginable pain…

Alex sprang into a sitting position on the bed. He used the edge of the sheet to wipe sweat and sleep from his eyes. Sunlight was streaming through a crack between his bedroom curtains. It had taken him a long time to fall asleep and all he'd gotten for his trouble was the same damned nightmare.

He looked around at the small apartment bedroom. He owned a real estate company, but had never bought his own house. No place had felt like home to him for thirteen years.

Alex rolled to his side and pressed the button on the answering machine. He listened to Lacey's message for, probably the hundredth time. "Hi Alex, I'm calling to let you know I got home safely." There was a pause. Had she wanted to say something and decided against it? Was she thinking about that scorching kiss, the way he had half the night?

"Have a good night," she finished before hanging up.

"To hell with it!" Alex threw off the covers. He'd take a quick shower and buy a cup of coffee on his way to Indian Lakes. It was time to start exorcizing this woman from his blackened soul.

Chapter Four

It was nearly noon when Lacey walked to the road to collect the mail. She and the kids had gone fishing after an early breakfast. Tonight's supper would be fresh catfish. They'd brought in six, cleaned and skinned on the boat. Now they were soaking in buttermilk. Everything else they'd caught had been thrown back into the lake for another day.

She didn't know why she'd kept so many fish. The three of them usually ate four. The kids were growing and had big appetites. They'd split the extra one. Maybe it was due to the guilt she felt over her argument with her grandfather. Her subconscious wanted to invite him for supper. Her conscious mind wasn't crazy about the idea.

The disparity with Granddad had started years ago and was a constant irritation. He was judgmental, opinionated, and unforgiving. She often worried about the influence he'd have over Jerrod. Clarence Carlyle wouldn't be her first choice for a male role model for her son. Thankfully, he and Jenna tended to avoid each other. Her daughter had learned at a young age that Granddad wasn't susceptible to female charm.

Despite her grumpy grandfather's opinion of their lifestyle, she and the kids loved the farm. It was exactly the life Lacey had wanted for Jerrod and Jenna; fresh air, wide-open spaces, and working with the earth and animals. If they had to give it up, she didn't know what she'd do. Perhaps she could sell off the livestock for the money to live on while she found some other kind of work. The young calves and piglets weren't worth much yet, but she wouldn't have a place to keep them soon anyway.

She refused to entertain the thought of marrying Alex. His motives were less than honorable. She'd already found out that his word couldn't be trusted. Those weren't even the most compelling reasons to keep him out of her life. The way he'd kissed her, the day before, had proved that her body still yearned for him. A man would just muck up her hectic life.

Lacey pulled a few envelopes from the roadside mailbox. She hoped for notice of an inheritance or a large sweepstakes prize. Instead, she found a bill from the electric company and another from the feed store.

Gravel crunched under slow moving tires on the road. Lacey used the envelopes to shade her eyes as she squinted in their direction. A silver BMW was approaching. "Son of a bitch," she murmured.

Alex let the car idle beside her as he lowered the window. "I'm glad to see you have a real mailbox now. It seems, from your claim, that the post office box wasn't very reliable."

"Granddad checked that box every day on his way home. We never noticed anything else missing." The pleasantness of the day had just ended. "What do you want, Alex?"

"Get in and I'll take you up to the house." He reached over and opened the passenger side door. "There's something I want to talk to you about."

"You could have called," Lacey said.

Alex ignored her statement. "Hey, I like your brand." He leaned into the steering wheel for a better view of the oval wooden sign above the gate. It had two capital Js overlapping in the center and a scalloped pattern on the border. It was burned into the wood, not painted. "What does it stand for?"

"You'll find out soon enough." Lacey slid into the car seat feeling like one of her catfish: caught, skinned, gutted, and waiting to be fried. It was best to get it over with. The kids were in the barn doing chores. She had a little time to sit down with him and explain. Two mischievous children were not part of his weekend plans. They would probably be the deal breaker. Yes, she wanted to break the deal. No, she didn't want to give up her farm.

Alex rolled to a stop when the house came into view. "I know this house," he said, surprised. "Mark Garvey lived here when we were kids. I used to sleep over with him all the time. His mom made the best peanut butter cookies in the world. I wonder what happened to good old Mark and his folks."

She wondered if Alex had noticed how rundown the house had gotten after all these years. She didn't have the resources Mr. Garvey had. Most of her money and energy went into the livestock and garden. Those were the things that fed her family and paid the bills.

"Mark moved to Atlanta, got married and had two kids," she told him. "His parents sold the place to move closer to them."

"Can you imagine that—Mark, a family man? He probably has an SUV with a big sloppy dog hanging out the window. I can see him now, driving the little monsters to soccer practice and ballet lessons."

Chuckling, he turned to Lacey. "You know, my brother Travis has two little girls. He's such a dope over them, but he always was a loser."

Lacey jumped out of the car leaving the door hanging open. She stomped across the lawn and up the steps to her front porch. She remembered Travis. He was a couple of years older than Alex. He wasn't as athletic or quite as good-looking, but he wasn't a loser. Being a good dad certainly didn't make him a loser. Who did Alex think he was, saying such a thing?

Alex closed both car doors and bounded up the steps behind her. She stopped and turned so suddenly, he ran into her. Why did he have to smell so good, feel so solid?

"Is there a reason you're here, Alex?"

"Yeah." He hesitated for a moment. "I wanted to talk to you about the wedding."

"There isn't going to be a wedding."

"Yes there is."

"You don't know anything about me or the life I have here."

A spark ignited in Alex's eyes. Lacey couldn't tell if it was lust or anger, but she feared it was both. She'd never seen that expression on his face before, but something told her to run. Before she could open the screen door, he grabbed her shoulders and pulled her against his chest.

"I know you, Lacey. And I know when those little wheels are turning in your head. You aren't going to run me off, and I'm not going to let you weasel your way out of this again. I'm not a kid and I don't have stars in my eyes anymore. You are going to belong to me if you want this farm to belong to you."

Belong to him? Lacey was barely able to gasp before his mouth crashed down on hers. In seconds, the hard punishing kiss turned passionate. She hadn't been kissed like this in…ever. She suddenly realized she was giving him his way. She should be angry, fighting, not melting like butter against his hard muscled chest. She tore her mouth away.

"What gives you the right to kiss me like that?" she demanded.

The spark in his eyes had grown into a raging fire. "You owe me a lot more than a few kisses and it's about time I started collecting. You'd better get used to the idea."

Lacey pushed her hands against his chest, but he didn't budge. "You'd actually force yourself on me? What kind of man have you become?"

"When the time comes, I won't have to force you. We both know it," he growled. "I'm not the only one who's grown up now."

When he kissed her again, Lacey wasn't sure if she was struggling to get away or get closer to him. She was consumed by heat inside and out. Neither of them heard the bottom step creak.

****

"You'd better let my mom go right now, mister, or I'll pound a hole in your head."

Alex spun around to find a gangly young boy three feet from his back. First, he saw the stubborn scowl under a mass of curly, sun streaked, dark auburn hair. Then he noticed the hammer the boy was bouncing in his right hand. Damn, this kid was serious.

Alex said the first thing that came to mind. "Who the hell are you?"

Lacey cleared her throat. "Alex, this is my son, Jerrod."

Still not releasing her, Alex swung his head back to look down at Lacey. "You have a kid?"

"Well, actually…" Before she could answer, another voice came from the side of the house.

"You want me to shoot him, Jerrod?"

To his left, there stood a skinny young girl wearing a cowboy hat and glaring at him from over the barrel of a shotgun. Indian Lakes had changed. It had its own little gang right here on Lacey's farm.

"You'd better not," Jerrod replied. "You'd get us all in your spray. You should have brought the twenty-two. Then I would've gladly let you plug him."

Lacey finally succeeded in wiggling out of Alex's grasp. "Jenna, you put that shotgun away. Mr. Benson is my guest and you're scaring him. I want you both to go inside and wash up for lunch."

Alex was awestruck. "You have two kids…and they carry weapons."

"Well, not usually," Lacey sighed. "You know how dangerous it can be, out in the country, snakes and gators and such."

"I do now!"

Alex followed Lacey through the house to the kitchen. He quietly sat at the end of an oblong wooden table while she put together peanut butter and jelly sandwiches. She was a mom. He just couldn't get his mind wrapped around the fact. She still looked as sweet and sexy as she had thirteen years ago. She sure as hell didn't look like someone's mother.

Lacey removed apples and carrots from the refrigerator and began washing them. No chips or cookies, just fruit and vegetables, proof positive, she was a mom. How could this have happened?

She'd been with another man. The thought hit Alex like a bolt of lightning. She'd said that she'd never married, but she'd given herself to another man and had his children. Alex didn't know much about kids, but the girl, Jenna, had to be nearing puberty. She was slightly shapely in an awkward way. The boy, Jerrod, was shorter, but not by much. That would mean Lacey had been involved with someone during the year he'd been stuck in the hospital. Her coldhearted betrayal was even worse than he thought. She'd thrown him over for another man.

He tried to remember all the guys he and Travis had gone to school with, and all the others in the class in between. Did any of them resemble Lacey's kids? Hell, he could barely remember his own name, let alone his old high school buddies. Besides that, the kids looked an awful lot like her.

Was the guy still in the picture? Did Lacey still have feelings for him? Of course she did. She wasn't the kind of girl who'd have kids with just anybody. He and Lacey had never even discussed having a family. She sure hadn't wasted any time after he'd left, though.

He was positive Lacey had said she'd never been married.

Alex had been aware of the way people treated Lacey years ago. He remembered what Miss Dell had said to her on the day her parents were buried, and how badly it hurt her. Her grandfather was harder on her than anyone, but he was all that kept some of the old biddies from tearing her apart. She hadn't been the bows and ruffles type they thought she should be. How had those small-minded women taken the news that she'd had a child out of wedlock, not once but twice?

His mind circled back to the thought of Lacey with another man. His blood boiled with jealousy. Did he have a right to be jealous? Hell yes! She'd promised herself to him.

Looking at her now, Alex knew he still wanted her. He wanted all she'd promised him. He wanted her heart and soul, if only for a little while. But he'd be damned before he'd admit it. Would two kids keep him from achieving his end game? He didn't know. Kids hadn't been part of the plan.

This was going to take a considerable amount of thought.

Chapter Five

Lacey was running on nervous energy. She kept her eyes on her task to avoid looking at Alex. He must have a hundred questions about the kids. Or more to the point, how she'd come to have them. He'd made it crystal clear in the car that he didn't care for children. Had he felt that way when they planned to be married? It was one subject out of many that they hadn't discussed, but should have. They'd barely been more than children themselves.

She filled two bowls with whole raw carrots and apples. Next, she wrapped the sandwiches in paper napkins to place on top. "Have you eaten? If you don't like peanut butter, I have bologna in the fridge."

"I haven't had a PB&J sandwich since I left Indian Lakes." Truthfully, he hadn't eaten anything since lunch the day before. His stomach was suddenly reminding him. "You can hold the carrots though. Do your kids actually eat that stuff? They must be half rabbit."

A smile tugged at Lacey's lips. "They eat lunch in the barn on the weekends. They give the horses some of the carrots and apples.

I've always suspected they were half animal. Exactly what kind is yet to be determined. Depending on their moods, they can be anything from cuddly bunnies to Tasmanian devils."

When Lacey placed two sandwiches in front of him, Alex grabbed her wrist. "Don't you think it would have been nice to mention that you had a couple of kids?"

Lacey felt like a deer in the crosshairs. With the touch of one hand he could make her heart pound and her mouth water for his. This had to stop. But before she could say anything, they were interrupted again. "What's going on?" Instead of wielding a hammer, Jerrod's hands were fisted at his sides. Jenna stood behind him with a confused look.

"Well, look whose back, Annie Oakley and Hammerman." Alex turned Lacey loose and raised his hands. "Don't shoot, we're just talking."

The tension between the two males was palpable.

"Mr. Benson is the new owner of the property," Lacey said. "I'm hoping we can reach an agreement that would allow us to stay here."

"Hell of a way to do business, mister." Jerrod growled.

"Watch your mouth, young man." Lacey filled the kid's hands with their lunches, and then led them to the back door by their collars. "Mr. Benson happens to be an old friend of mine. Go on out to the barn and I'll be there shortly to give you your afternoon chores."

"Maybe I ought to stay inside and keep an eye on your *friend*," Jerrod suggested.

Lacey held the door open. "We've got grown-up things to discuss and we don't need you underfoot."

Jerrod stared Alex down. "I think he has a lot more than business on his mind, Mom."

"I'm a grown woman, Jerrod. I can take care of myself."

"Yeah I know," Jerrod replied stubbornly, "but he already got you to kiss him like there was no tomorrow."

"Get out right now, son, before I tan your behind."

The twins stopped in the doorway. Jenna nudged Jerrod's shoulder with her own. He held his hand out, palm up. She shook her head. He tilted his chin up defiantly. She turned her face away and walked out the door.

When the back screen door slammed behind them, Lacey gave Alex a weak smile. She could feel the heat in her cheeks. Damn her redhead complexion. "I guess this is going to be a Tasmanian devil day."

"What the hell was that?" Alex asked.

"What?" Lacey went back to finish their sandwiches.

"That little dance the two of them did before they left."

"Oh." Shrugging, Lacey said, "They have a kind of sign language. They've done that since they were toddlers."

"What did they say?"

"I don't know."

Alex rolled his eyes and shook his head.

To gain a little privacy, she and Alex decided to have their lunch on the end of the dock.

Lacey studied Alex as they quietly ate their sandwiches. He looked comfortable in casual clothes. More like his old self. His feet dangled over the side in low socks and sneakers. Knee length khaki shorts revealed strong legs, lightly covered in silky dark hair. A long sleeved, striped shirt hung open over his black T-shirt. She hadn't been kissed by a man in long time.

He'd awaked feelings that had faded and been forgotten, feelings that had kept her awake most of the night.

He nudged her john-boat with his toe. "I'm surprised this old thing can still float."

"We took it out this morning and caught a mess of catfish for supper." Lacey was relieved to have a neutral subject to discuss.

"Any chance you'd have enough for a guest?"

Alex's shy smile was still as hard to resist as it had ever been. "As it happens, I do." Why had she said that? "I'm also making hushpuppies, coleslaw and green beans, fresh from the garden. I do have to warn you though, everybody works for their supper around here."

"Just tell me what to do," Alex offered excitedly. "I'm your slave for fresh catfish."

Lacey laughed. This just might be a good time to show him how her business ran. There were no days off when you relied on a farm for your living. If he was going to spend time here, he should be involved. Maybe some physical labor would change his mind about coming around.

"Okay. After lunch I'll have Jerrod get started on the front porch and you can help Jenna in the barn. If you do a good job, I might let you decide what we'll have for dessert tonight." Maybe an afternoon of horse manure would run him off.

"That shouldn't be too hard." Alex leaded back on his elbows. "As I recall, you only have three horses."

"I only own three horses. That doesn't include the four I board for people in town."

Suddenly Alex looked serious. "How do you do it,

Lacey? How do you make enough money to keep this place up and raise two children?"

"Every season I sell the older cattle and pigs for slaughter. There are always enough babies to take their place, and a few for our own use. I sell eggs from the hens and honey from the bees. The bees pollinate my garden and I sell vegetables from that. I board a few horses and give riding lessons. Everything here has a purpose. It isn't an easy life, but it's what we're used to, and it suits us." She purposely used the words we and us. He had to understand that she was part of a package deal. That would surely dissuade him.

"How did you get into all this? I know it wasn't your grandfather's idea." Alex wore an expression of awe.

"Do you remember old Mrs. Plumber who had a little farm out on County Line Road?"

"I sure do," Alex laughed. "She caught Travis and me stealing oranges from her grove when I was ten. She made us weed her garden until it got too dark to see. We got in trouble for coming in late that night, but at least our dad didn't know we'd stolen the oranges."

"She was tough, all right," Lacey admitted before continuing her story. "She hired me to keep house for her when the kids were toddlers. It was the only job I could find that would allow me to take them along. I'd learned farming from my parents, but she taught me the business end of it. I was saving the money to rent a place of my own. The kids had started school when she was placed in a nursing home. Her farm was sold to pay her bills, but she gave me all of her livestock, supplies, and equipment to start my own farm. The poor woman didn't have any family of her own."

"What about Jenna and Jerrod's father?" Alex asked.

Lacey's heart leapt into her throat. She was glad Alex was looking out at the water and not at her. "What do you mean?"

"Does he help you out, financially I mean?" Alex turned, examining her expression. "Does he come around much?"

"No." Lacey could barely answer past the lump in her throat. "He took off a long time ago. I do just fine on my own."

She stood and brushed the dust off the seat of her shorts. Gathering the disposable plates and cups from their lunch gave her an excuse not to look him in the eye. "You can help Jenna with the stalls while I work with Jerrod on the front porch. It's hot, dirty work. You may want to take off that extra shirt."

Alex's lips tightened. "I'll be fine as I am."

****

The one thing Alex hated most was having his scars exposed. On the few occasions when he'd been coaxed into taking off his long sleeved shirt, he'd regretted it. Strangers looked at him with disgust or fear, but what hurt more were the people closest to him. Friends and family members' eyes would fill with pity. They'd quickly look away and grope for a safe subject to discuss rather than deal with his deformity. Women he'd been interested in would find an excuse to distance themselves from him, as though the scars were contagious. He hadn't had a real relationship since the accident. Since Lacey.

He was a healthy, heterosexual male and sometimes the urge would have to be satiated by someone besides himself. He'd tried prostitutes a few times, but the experience was impersonal and degrading.

Now, he occasionally visited out of town bars late in the evening. He wouldn't approach an inebriated woman—that was against his morals—but he wouldn't turn down what was offered. They'd have rushed interludes in bathroom stalls, storage rooms or the back seat of a car. Anywhere as long as it was dark and total nudity wasn't required. On his way home, he'd toss their phone numbers out his car window along with his dignity.

He hadn't held a woman skin-to-skin since his last time with Lacey. Maybe that was the reason for his obsession. He still craved that time in the afterglow when two lovers connected mind, body and soul, the way it had been with her.

The smell of horse manure, leather, and straw pulled his mind back to the present.

Both children were silently working at their separate tasks. Jenna moved the horses, one at a time, into the corral while Jerrod stacked six-foot planks of wood across a wheelbarrow. They hadn't been told specifically what to do, they just knew what had to be done. They were hard workers. If he were their father he'd be proud. Too many kids never got off the sofa these days or put down their game station controllers and cell phones.

Watching them, it suddenly occurred to Alex that if Jenna were older, she could have been his. She would have been his excuse to stay. His life wouldn't have gone to shit.

No, that wasn't true. Lacey had been the best thing

that had ever happened to him and he'd still left. With a kid on the way, he would have been more determined to try to find his fortune.

"You may want to get a pair of work gloves from the tack room," Jerrod sneered. "I imagine your hands are pretty tender."

"Don't worry about me." Alex started raking through the first stall with a pitchfork. He wished the boy would get over his surliness. It had gone from annoying to irritating. "What are you going to do with all that wood?"

"We fixed a hole in the porch roof last week. The hole had caused the floor to rot out at one end." Jerrod pushed the full wheelbarrow toward the door. Before leaving, he added, "You might have noticed when you came in, if you hadn't been assaulting my mother."

Alex watched him walk away and thanked all that was holy he hadn't been asked to help the sour little shit. What had put such a big chip on his shoulder?

He went back to work steadily cleaning out each stall. He'd show that kid he wasn't a greenhorn. He'd been raised here in Indian Lakes too. He knew his way around a barn.

Jenna's voice surprised him a few minutes later. "Have you known my mom long, Mr. Benson?" He hadn't heard her return because of the sawing and hammering noises coming from the house.

"I've known her for as long as I can remember," Alex said. "I grew up here in Indian Lakes. Your mom was a year behind me in school. Our parents played cards every Wednesday night."

Jenna used a rake to spread the hay on the floor of the stall he'd just finished. "I wish I'd known my grandparents. Mom talks about them all the time. She really misses them. Granddad is such a grumpy old grouch, but don't tell Mom I said so."

Alex remembered well.

"She needs friends her own age that she can talk to, you know?" Jenna continued. "She's lonely a lot of the time. Jerrod and I are always here for her, but sometimes there are things she can't talk to us about."

Alex sensed that Jenna was trying to get somewhere with her line of conversation. "What kinds of things?"

"I don't know…maybe she'd like to talk about my dad. Did you know him?"

Alex stopped to look at Jenna, but she kept right on working, not making eye contact. "Honey, I don't know who your dad is."

"That makes two of us." Jenna sighed deeply. "Mom says she's not ready to open that can of worms yet. She says that if he knew about us he'd love us, but I find that hard to believe. If he didn't love Mom enough to stay with her, he can't be a very nice man."

Alex moved on to the next stall. "Jenna, I don't mean to make a bad situation worse, but you're a big girl, so I have to ask. How can a man not know he has two children? One maybe, but not two."

Jenna's smile was so much like Lacey's, full and bright. "Jerrod and I are twins, silly. Mom says Jerrod is still small because he hasn't hit puberty yet. He really hates it when she says things like that."

Their conversation was interrupted by a loud crack followed by a shrill, painful scream. His only thought was of the old shotgun he'd seen that morning. He threw his pitchfork to the ground and raced out of the barn.

Chapter Six

Alex followed the sound of Lacey's screams. His heart pounded like a jackhammer. The physical exertion wasn't a problem. He usually ran three miles in the morning before work. But this quick jaunt across the lawn seemed like running the Boston marathon.

"Everything's okay, Lacey, it's going to be all right," he shouted.

How the hell did he know? He didn't even know what was happening. He said it because he needed to take control. He needed to alleviate her fear. He was the man, dammit.

He found Lacey kneeling behind Jerrod at the end of the porch. She had her hands under the boy's arms as he sat on the floor. She was tugging on him with all her might. Jerrod wasn't budging. Alex was confused by Jerrod's stubbornness, until he realized that one of his legs had gone hip-deep into the floor. He pushed Lacey away from her son to assess the problem.

Two rotted boards had been pulled up and thrown aside. They'd been replaced by the fresh wood Jerrod had brought from the barn. The hammer and an overturned box of three-inch nails indicated the job was still in progress. Jerrod's leg had broken through one of the remaining old boards.

"I can't get him out." Lacey's eyes were filled with panic. "He's too heavy for me and his leg is really stuck. How am I going to get him out of there?"

Alex knelt beside Jerrod and looked closer at the area his leg had gone through. It was a good thing Lacey hadn't succeeded in pulling the boy out. The jagged edge of the board was embedded in the back of his thigh.

"Flex your ankle and tell me if you think your leg is broken," he instructed Jerrod.

Jerrod grimaced. A tear sprang from each eye and cut through the dust and sweat on his cheeks. He didn't make a sound, but he shook his head, teeth clamped tightly.

Jenna stood nearby. Her hands shook and her face was deathly white. She looked as though she might get sick, or worse, go into shock.

"You see, Jenna," Alex said gently. "Everything is going to be fine. It would really help a lot if you would get a wash cloth, towel, soap, and some warm water to take to Jerrod's room. Can you do that, honey?"

Jenna nodded her head jerkily and rushed inside.

"What can I do to help?" Lacey asked.

"Cover his bed with a clean sheet or blanket." Alex looked around, his mind forming a plan. "We'll need topical ointment, bandages, and probably tweezers. I'll get him loose and take him upstairs."

Lacey didn't question him, she just ran inside the house to gather the items.

Alex spotted a saw on the planks of wood still on the wheelbarrow. He decided it would be a slow and painful process to use it. No matter what he did it was going to hurt like hell. It would be better to get it done quickly.

As soon as Lacey and Jenna were out of sight, Alex

stripped off his shirt and stuffed it around Jerrod's trapped leg. With four swift blows of the hammer the rotten board that held the boy captive was in chunks.

When he looked up to see how Jerrod had faired, he found the boy staring at his scarred arm with an intense expression. "Geez! That had to hurt."

Jerrod seemed to find the damage interesting rather than repulsive. Alex had never gotten that reaction before. "Yeah, it sure did." He chuckled in response. He stood and gripped Jerrod's hand to pull him to his feet. When he bent forward to take Jerrod over his shoulder, the boy balked.

"You're not going to carry me," he declared.

"You won't make it up those stairs fast enough to keep from bleeding all over the place." Alex didn't feel like wrestling the boy, and Jerrod looked ready to fight. "I'll give you a choice. You can go over my shoulder in a fireman's carry or I'll cradle you in my arms like a baby. One way or the other, I'm taking you upstairs. What's it going to be?"

Jerrod agreed to lean over Alex's shoulder. Alex bounded up the stairs as quickly as he could. Jerrod grunted with every bounce, but it couldn't be helped.

After laying Jerrod face down on his bed, Alex looked around at the NASCAR posters on the walls. He'd never taken the time from his busy schedule to watch a NASCAR race. He didn't know anything about the drivers. Maybe if he'd had a son, he would have made the time.

Why was he thinking about something like that? Kids weren't part of his plan.

Lacey and Jenna had brought the items he'd asked for, but only Lacey remained in the room. She leaned over Jerrod and began working the belt loose from his shredded jeans.

"Do you want me to handle this, Lacey?"

"No, Mom!" Jerrod cried out.

"I can handle it." Lacey gave Alex a feeble smile. "Thanks for all your help, though. I'm usually pretty good in a crisis. I only tend to fall apart when it involves one of the kids. It's a mom thing."

Alex walked slowly back down the stairs. He paused by the two pictures that hung halfway down on the wall. They were old school pictures of Jenna and Jerrod. Each of them had been a lot smaller with messy hair and missing front teeth.

At the bottom of the stairs was a wicker clothesbasket. Inside were three pairs of worn sneakers, two baseball gloves, a bat, and a Frisbee with teeth marks around the edge.

Most of the living room furniture was older than he was, but it was clean and comfortable looking. This house was a home. He'd practically shoved his way into it with the express purpose of turning it upside down. He hadn't considered what might be inside.

He couldn't allow himself to worry about that. He'd waited thirteen years to get retribution. And besides that, his presence here wouldn't have any impact on the children. He'd just make it a point to avoid them.

He stepped onto the front porch and suddenly Jenna was there. Her arms wrapped around him tighter than a tourniquet. "I'm so glad you're here, Mr. Benson. I don't know what we would have done without you."

Alex sat with her and ran his hand down her thick

braid. Without the cowboy hat he saw that her hair was also auburn, a medium shade between Lacey's bright copper and Jerrod's dark rust. He remembered Lacey at this stage. That was about the time she'd first caught his eye in a new and mysterious way. He wondered how many boys in school were looking at Lacey's little girl that way now.

"No worries, sweetheart." When had he started using pet names like that? He didn't feel much like himself today. "Your brother is tougher than buffalo hide. He'll be running around and making trouble in no time."

Without backing away, Jenna ran her hand down Alex's left arm. He'd forgotten to cover it. Now, his long sleeved overshirt was a bloody mess. He realized that no one, absolutely not one single person, outside of medical professionals, had ever touched him there. What was with these kids? Alex stiffened: he couldn't help it.

"You must be awfully tough too, Mr. Benson. Getting burned like this had to be horrible," Jenna exclaimed. "Does it still hurt or anything?"

Alex tried to relax under Jenna's scrutiny, but it was hard. "It's a little sensitive sometimes, but no, it doesn't really hurt anymore."

****

By the time Lacey could leave Jerrod, more than an hour had passed. She felt as though she'd removed enough wood from the child's leg to build a new barn. Actually, it wouldn't have covered the bottom of a tea cup.

Exhaustion had finally taken him into a deep sleep. Lacey wished she could take a nap as well, but the chores were behind schedule and now she was shorthanded. When she stepped out the front door, she found Alex measuring a plank of wood to be cut. All the old boards at the damaged end of the porch had been removed. She realized they should have started the job that way. Maybe then, her son wouldn't be upstairs with the skin scraped off the back of his leg. She was relieved not to have to see the hole he'd fallen into.

Alex sawed six-inches off one end of a board. He had a rag tied around his head to keep the sweat from dripping into his eyes. His black T-shirt was soaked and clinging to his wide chest. The muscles in his arms glistened as they flexed, even his left arm. It was hairless and marbled with burn scars, not quite as thick as the right one. Still, he was the sexiest man she'd ever seen.

Alex walked to the end of the porch and slid the freshly cut board into place.

"I'll nail while you cut." Lacey picked up Jerrod's discarded hammer and a handful of nails. She'd found out that if you live in a sixty-year-old house, you'd better know your tools and be willing to use them.

"How's the boy?" Alex shouted over the pounding.

"Tired, humiliated and hurting." Lacey crawled closer to add a few nails further down the board. "Kids have an amazing ability of bouncing back fast, though. He'll be as right as rain in a week."

"You'll have to keep that wound clean and he'll need something for pain soon. That leg is going to be sore and stiff. Maybe he should see a doctor."

"This job doesn't come with benefits, Alex." She looked up. "I'll take him to the free clinic if infection sets in."

"This is a hard life for a woman and two kids," Alex remarked. "Maybe a regular job with benefits would be a good idea."

Lacey sat up straighter. "It's a hard life for anyone, but it's the life I've chosen." Her chin raised in stubborn determination. "People think of Florida and imagine palm trees and sandy beaches. They don't realize that we raise beef cattle and train rodeo horses. They don't know that we grow more than oranges. Not very long ago, Florida was the second largest dairy producing state in the country. Now all the farmland is being bought up for theme parks, retirement condominiums, and ranchettes. The rich tourists and snow birds own us."

Alex returned to sawing without saying a word. Lacey felt a twinge of guilt. Maybe this hadn't been a good time to admonish his plans. He had just helped her son.

She hammered in another nail and then nodded toward his arm. "I guess you'd know something about medical treatment. It looks like you've had quite a bit of it, yourself. You want to tell me how that happened?"

She could tell by his hesitation that he didn't want to talk about it, but he gave in and answered anyway. "There was an explosion aboard ship. One of the engineers was killed. I was in the gangway outside of the room." Alex paused, and then added, "There's more to it than just my arm. It was pretty bad. Does it bother you?"

"I know it bothers you for me to see it, but it shouldn't. It's just a part of you, a part of your history." Lacey began hammering again.

"You know, most people are grossed out by it. You and your kids act like it's no worse than a scratch. I don't get it."

"Well, a lot of people are idiots," Lacey told him. "When you work in this business you can't be squeamish. We have animals attacking each other, having accidents, and being born deformed. They're often turned out by the others to fend for themselves or die. Sometimes we get to them in time to help, sometimes not."

"Well, that little story really brightens my day," Alex grumbled.

"The moral of the story is: we're not animals," her voice lowered. "Although, you may not have guessed by the way my children behave."

Alex measured, cut and placed another board before he spoke again. "You once said I was perfect. As you can see, I'm not perfect anymore."

Lacey's eyes narrowed in contemplation. "Oh, I get it. You thought I was referring to your looks. No, I was talking about your batting stance. Yeah, definitely, you had a great swing."

It was nice to hear Alex laugh again.

Chapter Seven

Lacey was lost in her thoughts as the beans boiled in a pot with bacon and the fish sizzled in the big iron skillet.

The sight of Alex's injured arm bothered her more then she'd let on. Not for the reason that he'd expected, though. She knew that the accident must have been horrendous, followed by fear, pain and a long recovery. It saddened her to think of Alex suffering through that alone. Thank God he hadn't lost his arm, or even worse, his life. It had taken every bit of willpower she had not to throw her arms around him and try to give him comfort.

She'd seen the way he carefully hid the scars. Whether he knew it or not, part of the pain was still with him. He seemed like such a confident man on the outside. Inside he was hiding a terrible insecurity.

They'd each gone through their own hell in the last thirteen years. It had changed the people they used to be, and yet, she still felt drawn to him. The truth was she didn't want to miss him anymore. She'd learned to bury it long ago, but she'd never gotten over him.

Now that he knew most of her secrets, he'd give up the idea of marriage. She'd more than likely lose the Double J. But the one thing that could never be replaced was people. She wanted to keep Alex in her life. They'd only be friends now; too much water had passed under the bridge. But friends were priceless. She'd keep the memories of that month they'd been lovers like she always had, locked away in a secret place.

"Are you all right, Mom? You look a little spaced out."

Lacey went back to stirring the hushpuppy mix. "I'm fine, Jenna. It's just hot in this kitchen and I've had a long day. I appreciate you getting all the chores done. That helped a lot."

"It was Mr. Benson's idea." Jenna filled a glass with water and sipped it as she leaned on the counter next to her mother. "He said we needed to stay out of your way while you took care of Jerrod. He helped me with a lot of it. He really is a nice man."

"You seem to be getting along with him," Lacey said. "I wish your brother would make an effort to be a little friendlier."

"Jerrod's just been all puffed up, playing *man-of-the-house*. It really threw him for a loop when we caught you two kissing. It kind of surprised me too. Sorry about the shotgun and all, but you have to admit it's kind of funny, looking back on it now. I've already apologized to Mr. Benson. He's really a great guy, you know. He's handsome too. Is that what you were thinking about when I came in? Don't you think he's hot, Mom? You could do worse, you know."

"Jenna, you just met the man a few hours ago!" Lacey turned away to hide the blush that was scalding her cheeks. Hell yes, she thought he was hot. "Go up and get ready for supper, and tell your brother to do the same."

Jenna skipped up the stairs. God save her from

52

young girls with romance on their minds.

****

Alex sat down to the best home cooked meal he'd had in many years. The catfish could melt in your mouth and the hushpuppies were light and crispy. Lacey had used her mother's recipe for the coleslaw. It was creamy, not sour, the way northern people made it. On the counter sat a picture perfect key lime pie. After all the chaos that day, she'd found time to make a pie and remembered that key lime was his favorite.

He found Jenna to be utterly amusing and charming, but he didn't know how she was able to eat, as much as she talked. She had a million questions for him about Orlando, and mostly, Disney World. He was amazed to learn they'd never been there. It wasn't right for native Floridians to pass through childhood without meeting Mickey Mouse. He made a personal commitment to himself to take them as soon as Jerrod's leg healed. He'd been there when he took employees for company outings. It might be fun to see it from a kid's perspective. He was finding it hard to avoid the kids as he'd planned. This farm revolved around them. They were the biggest part of Lacey's life.

At the other side of the table Jerrod picked at the food on his plate. Lacey must have noticed too.

"You're awfully quiet tonight, Jerrod. Is your leg hurting worse?" she asked.

Jerrod glared at Alex as he answered. "My leg isn't the problem, I just don't care for all the changes going on around here."

Lacey looked across the table to Alex, and then lowered her eyes to her plate. "Nothing's changed that I know of."

"You've changed," Jerrod accused. "Since when did you start kissing men right in front of the house? You're getting to be no better than Casey's mom. Maybe all those people in town are right about you. Next thing I know, you'll be wearing short skirts, high heels and tons of makeup. You'll start staying out to all hours of the night in bars. God only knows who you'll be dragging home with you next."

Lacey stood so quickly, her chair clattered to the floor behind her. Her open hand shot out to slap Jerrod hard across his cheek. In the next second she looked devastated. She'd probably never touched the kid in anger. Given the opportunity, Alex could have kicked his skinny butt and not regretted it a bit.

A sob tore through Lacey's throat as she ran out the back door. Both kids sat in stunned silence. They visibly jumped when the screen door slammed behind her.

Alex stood with the palms of his hands on the table. He leaned toward Jerrod with a menacing expression. "Jenna, could you leave your brother and me alone for a moment."

"I-I don't know," she stammered.

"Don't worry, I won't kill him. If he gives me any trouble, I'll just make him wish he were dead."

"Yes, sir."

Jenna turned to her brother, raised both hands and made a pecking motion with her head, like a chicken. In return, Jerrod raised his hands and shook them rapidly. Jenna took on a superior smug expression and walked out of the room.

This sign language of theirs would take some getting used to. Alex took a few deep breaths before he spoke. "You were so out of line just then, young man. Your mother works too hard to have to put up with crap like that."

"I don't have to listen to you," Jerrod sneered. "You're nobody to me and you don't even belong here. I'm going to my room."

"Is that the best you've got...really?" Alex repositioned his feet and leaned closer. His nose was only six inches from Jerrod's. "Let me fill in the parts you forgot. I'm twice your size, I'm five times stronger, I'm ten times meaner, and I could take you out with both hands tied behind my back. Now let me tell you how this is going to go. I'm going to find your mom and bring her back here so you can give her the most sincere and heartfelt apology she's ever heard. If your butt moves out of that chair before that happens, I'll chase you down. Makes you think about that bum leg, doesn't it? Is there anything I've said that you don't understand, you little monster?"

****

Lacey let her legs dangle over the end of the dock. The pink twilight sky made the surface of the lake look like a sheet of lavender tinted glass. If she had to leave the Double J, the lake was what she'd miss most. She'd never lived in a place where she couldn't see the water from her window. But she'd decided that if she did have to move, it would be to a new town. She'd make a fresh start. She'd go to a place where people didn't know every detail of her past. Her kids shouldn't have to hear gossip about her.

Jerrod was clearly ashamed of her. That had been the worst pain she'd ever experienced. Then, to solidify his low opinion of her, she'd struck him. She wished she'd never gotten out of bed that morning.

Alex's footsteps sounded on the wooden planks' but she didn't turn around. She was too embarrassed. He sat on the corner of the dock with his back against the rail post, facing her right side.

"If you're thinking of jumping in the lake to end it all, let me know in advance." He stretched out his legs and crossed his ankles. "These shoes set me back a couple hundred bucks. I'd want a chance to take them off before I dive in after you. There's also my wallet and cell phone to consider."

Alex always could make her smile.

"I've never heard Superman complain about having his cape dry-cleaned," she replied. "I've never seen Batman ask for time to remove his utility belt. The Incredible Hulk never asks for a safety pin. If you're going to be a hero, you've got to be tough."

Alex's eyes widened. "So that's who you've been dating since I've been gone."

Lacey shook her head. "You can tell by the way my kids reacted to you that my social life is fairly nonexistent. After today, I plan to keep it that way."

"Well, if you're off the market, maybe I should check out Casey's mom. Do I know her? Is she cute?"

Lacey became serious. "I'm ashamed of Jerrod for talking about her that way. Donna Sullivan is a nice girl, trying to raise a kid on her own. She moved here a couple of years ago. The only job she could find was at the Road House, waiting tables at night. It hardly pays enough to make ends meet. And sometimes she looks for love in the wrong places. As you know, I've got my own reputation in this town, so I don't judge her."

Alex lowered his voice. "Where do you look for

love, Lacey?"

"I don't waste my time." Lacey responded too quickly. It was the truth. She mostly kept to herself.

Alex paused in thought. "I suppose you're waiting for Prince Charming to show up. If he does, you'll have to move the compost pile behind the barn. He'll need a place to stable his white steed, and royals have very sensitive noses."

Lacey smacked his shoulder.

"Take it easy, slugger. You've got a nasty right cross."

As soon as the words were out of his mouth, Lacey recalled the scene in the kitchen and felt her eyes fill with tears. "I don't know what came over me in there. I swear I've never hit one of my children before tonight. I've got to be the world's most horrible mom."

"You and Jerrod have both been under a lot of stress today, mostly because of me." Alex scooted closer and put his arm around her shoulders. "I'm sorry. I shouldn't have just shown up the way I did."

"That's no reason for Jerrod to bait me the way he has today. It's just not like him. You can ask anybody in Indian Lakes. He's normally a great kid." It was so easy to lean into Alex's warm shoulder. What would it be like to have this comfort all the time? Lacey couldn't afford to entertain that thought.

"Oh, I believe you, but you need to look at this from his point of view." Alex tightened his hold on her. "Face it, sweetheart. Those kids didn't miss the heat coming off the two of us, when they found us kissing. I was at the edge of my control. And I'm a stranger to them. Jenna thinks it was romantic, but Jerrod feels like he has to protect you. He'd like to punch my lights out, but he knows he's too small. Then, to add insult to injury, he fell through the porch and hurt himself. I heard him scream and saw him cry-big ego buster, babe. To top that off, I had to carry him to his room."

Lacey hadn't realized how degrading all that must have been for her son. "What am I going to do?"

Alex stood and offered Lacey a hand up. They began walking back to the house. "Let me come back next weekend. Jerrod's leg should be better by then. I could help him with his chores and spend some time with him. If we both live though the weekend, maybe we'll start being friends."

"You, here, for the whole weekend?" Lacey was astounded by Alex's suggestion. A man in her house overnight? A smoking hot, built for sex, kind of man? What would people say? She should say no, but she couldn't make the words come out. Instead, she changed the subject. "I can't believe that your taking up for Jerrod after the day we've had. You don't even like kids!"

"Yeah, I know." Alex shrugged. "Go figure. Maybe I'm trying to make points with the kid in order to get close to his sexy mom."

Lacey laughed until she opened the back door and saw her somber son, still sitting at the kitchen table.

"Mom, there's a few things I want to say before you start in on me," Jerrod began. "I know I was a jerk, and I hurt your feelings. I'm sorry I made you cry. And I'm not saying that 'cause of Mr. Benson. I mean it. You're the greatest mom ever."

"Thanks Jerrod." Lacey sat in the chair across from him. "You know, Mr. Benson and I were friends from the time we were just babies. We went to school together, and then he went into the Navy. Now that he's back, I'd like to spend some time with him. I was hoping to show him what great kids I've got, but that hasn't worked out very well today. He reminded me, outside, that you've had a pretty bad day. He offered to come back next weekend so he can help with your work. He seems to think you're a pretty tough guy. I guess I hadn't realized how much you're growing up, but make no mistake, you were wrong to talk to me the way you did. I was also wrong to hit you and I'm sorry. Now, if you give me a big hug, I just might cut that pie."

****

Alex hadn't followed Lacey inside. She'd needed time to straighten things out with her boy. But he'd been leaning against the siding under the kitchen window and heard their conversation. He straightened to walk around to the door.

Lacey was a hell of a mom. He actually wished he had a home and family like this one. Who was he kidding? He wanted this one. He decided there and then, he was going to marry Lacey Carlyle, kids and all. This is what had been missing from his life.

Chapter Eight

Lacey couldn't sleep. She'd hardly slept all week. She'd never had an overnight guest in her house past the age of twelve. Knowing Alex lay sleeping on her sofa brought back too many memories. She thought back to that June, so long ago, when they'd swim in the lake and then make love like there'd be no tomorrow. Then he'd nap on the blanket in the grass. She'd watch him breathe and memorized ever inch of his long lean body. She'd been completely fascinated by his masculine form. He'd been her first, and even though she'd lacked experience, he'd been her best. Perhaps her subconscious had known he'd be gone from her life too soon.

She still couldn't believe he was back. It was like walking into a dream. She didn't have to resist him, she was a grown woman, and heaven knows she had needs, needs he'd awakened in her. But how could she be sure he'd still be here the next day? The old memories were bad enough. She couldn't stand to miss him like that again.

Lacey stepped out of her room. It was the only bedroom on the left side of the stairs. The second bedroom on that side had been converted into an upstairs bathroom by the Garveys.

She tiptoed to the other side to check on the twins.

Jenna was sound asleep. Lacey had a theory that

the girl expended so much energy during the day she had to have a full night's sleep to recharge. Her system would shut down by ten and wouldn't reboot until six in the morning.

Jerrod, on the other hand, was restless. He'd toss and turn until his sheets were in a knot on the floor. She supposed his energy was infinite. Earlier in the night, she'd heard him get up a few times and walk down the stairs and back. Now, he was finally sleeping as well.

When she passed the top of the stairs, to return to her own room, she heard a strange noise from below. It sounded like a growl. The dogs never slept inside. Could some other animal have gotten into the house? She followed the sound down the stairs and into the living room.

She hadn't wanted to see Alex sleeping. She'd resisted it all night. But she couldn't ignore that noise. Alex lay on his right side on the sofa. His right hand reaching over, softly batted at his left arm. His brow was furrowed as he growled deeply and continually. He was dreaming about the fire.

Lacey quietly approached him. She knelt on the floor by the sofa and took his right hand in hers. She stroked his left arm.

"Shhh," she whispered. "Everything's going to be okay. You're okay."

He grabbed her hand in both of his. "Promise you'll tell her." His eyes were still closed. He was still dreaming. "Tell her I love her. Tell her I need her," he said in a garbled plea. He brought her hand to his strong, wide chest. "Lacey…"

After an hour, he hadn't made another sound. It had been hard to resist lying next to him, holding him.

Lacey slipped her hand from his and went to bed. She knew she wouldn't sleep, but she didn't want Alex or the twins finding her there in the morning.

****

Alex woke on Lacey's sofa with the sun streaming through the lace curtains. He couldn't remember the last time he'd slept so soundly. He supposed it was due to the fresh country air. He'd get plenty of that today. There was a lot that needed to be done, good old-fashioned physical labor.

Alex was no stranger to the gym. He worked out twice a week. Also, he ran at least four mornings a week, depending on his schedule. But it would feel good to actually work with his hands again. Fixing the front porch the week before had whetted his appetite for physical, constructive, outdoor activity. Besides that, he was tired of Jerrod's implications that he couldn't handle real work. It was time to show the boy what a man could do.

As he staggered to the bathroom, he caught the aroma of fresh brewed coffee. He desperately wanted a cup of that coffee.

Alex brushed his teeth and shaped his beard. He changed out of the running shorts and T-shirt he'd slept in. He didn't own a pair of pajamas, but it wouldn't do to sleep in the buff on the family's sofa.

He thought about Lacey. He hoped he'd have a few minutes alone with her before the kids got up. For as long as he'd known her, he'd never seen her first thing in the morning. He had a theory that you could tell the most about a woman by what she was like when she woke. A woman tended to lower her guard after a cozy night between the sheets. Would she be soft and drowsy, or coarse and grumpy? Did she wear frilly nightgowns or warm pajamas? There was a lot he wanted to learn about Lacey Carlyle, only in order to break through her barriers, of course.

Alex was still a few feet from the kitchen door when he realized Lacey wasn't alone and hadn't just woken up. Dammit, it was early Saturday morning. Didn't kids sleep in on the weekends? Despite the allure of the coffee, Alex hung back a moment to listen.

"Are you sure everything is finished?" Lacey asked.

"Yes, ma'am. All four legged creatures are feeling fat and happy." Jerrod seemed to be in a better mood this morning.

"The two legged ones should be feeling about the same." Lacey chuckled. "You two have put away more biscuits and gravy than any two truck drivers I know."

"We've probably put in more work than most truck drivers," Jerrod replied. "And, we still have a lot left to do. When is that lazy friend of yours going to haul his butt off the sofa?"

"Jerrod!"

That's when Alex decided to make his presence known. He lightly stepped backward down the hall and began whistling as he approached the kitchen a second time. "Morning everybody! I can't believe I didn't hear you get up. I'm usually a light sleeper, but all this fresh country air must have really put me under. What smells so good?"

"Mom made sausage gravy and biscuits this morning." Jenna jumped out of her chair. "Can I make you a plate?"

"I don't usually eat right away, but I'd love a cup

of coffee," Alex said. "Can you make me a cup with three sugars and no cream? I need a strong jolt to get me started in the morning."

Lacey and Jenna looked at each other with surprise and then laughed. Jenna clued him in to the joke. "Jerrod takes his coffee the same way. At least the two of you have one thing in common."

"We'll have plenty of time to compare notes," Alex informed her. "I've got the whole weekend off. And, since Jerrod has a bad leg, I'm going to help him with his chores."

Jenna pushed her bottom lip out in a pout. "I'll be stuck in the house all day, cleaning and doing laundry. I wish I could get some help, and then I could go outside with you guys."

"Sorry." Jerrod snatched an apple and bit into it. With his mouth full, he added, "Daylight's burning and if we helped you we wouldn't get everything done."

Alex turned to Jerrod. "By the way, how's that leg feeling?"

"It's a little stiff, but I'll live. When you work on a farm, you can't let a thing like that keep you down. We can't afford time off, like soft desk jockeys from the city."

The day was harder to get through than Alex expected. It wasn't because of the work, although the work seemed to never end. They'd painted the porch and shutters, hoed a two-acre garden, and cleaned the carburetor on a small tractor that Alex guessed was about as old as he was.

They only took a break long enough to eat lunch. Jerrod had packed cheese sandwiches and bottled water. Alex knew the boy was trying to make him miserable, but it would take a lot more than a cheese sandwich. He also knew Jerrod wanted to keep him away from Lacey. That wasn't working either. They could see the horse pens from everywhere they went. The pens were located between the house and barn, and in front of the garden.

Watching her was the hard part; or rather the way Lacey distracted him. Seeing her work with her horses was a thing of beauty. She exercised each one and only saddled the boarded horses. Seeing her straddle the bare backs of the sleek powerful animals, her bottom bouncing, her skin glowing with perspiration, gave him ideas he didn't need right then. Several times, while racing them back and forth between barrels, she'd come so close to the ground his heart nearly stopped. His stomach leapt into his throat every time she flew over an obstacle. He had to keep reminding himself that she knew what she was doing. This was her job. She didn't need him. It was a relief when she'd finished grooming the horses and returned them to their stalls.

****

Lacey had worked the horses harder than she needed to. She'd used them to pull herself away from the gravitational draw to Alex. Every time she'd looked up he'd been watching with lust filled eyes. The distraction made her work twice as hard in order to concentrate. Now that she could slow down, she felt boneless with fatigue.

Alex and Jerrod must have worn themselves out as well. They'd fallen asleep in front of the television as soon as supper was over.

She'd sent Jerrod to his room and Jenna followed soon after. Now she was spending the best part of a second night soothing away Alex's nightmares.

She wondered if this was a problem for him all the time or if it had been brought on by the past coming back to haunt him. If she wasn't losing so much sleep caring for him, she might be having nightmares as well. No, her dreams would probably be just the opposite. They'd probably be more of the erotic variety. Alex was proving hard to resist. She just couldn't decide why she was resisting. She knew they'd be explosive together. Maybe it was the fear of him leaving again.

Chapter Nine

Lacey and Alex followed the kids as far as the front porch. When an old white church bus pulled to a stop in the drive and beeped its horn, Jenna gave her mom a quick hug, and then hugged Alex as well. Jerrod didn't say good-bye at all. He shouted to a couple of friends he saw through the windows of the bus and ran to join them.

"I hope I didn't keep you from attending services." Alex returned the wave Jenna sent from her window.

"No, I don't usually go," Lacey informed him. "Indian Lake society and I don't mix well."

"I guess we have the house to ourselves for a while." Alex placed his hands on Lacey's waist and pulled her against him.

Lacey pushed away. She didn't look him in the eye when she spoke. "Alex, I'm not in the habit of falling into bed with men at the drop of a hat. I know we have a history, but that was a long time ago. Besides that, things have changed. I can't see you holding me to your ridiculous agreement, now that you know I have children."

Alex was stunned by Lacey's coolness. He thought he was making headway with her. Was it the kids or something else? His intentions hadn't had anything to do with their agreement or the kids, but if that was the game she wanted to play he could be just as cool.

"So, you're just going to give up? Just because you're a mother doesn't mean you have to act like my mother. What about your farm? You're willing to just walk away from it to save your virtue? You've already lost that battle. Virtue goes hand-in-hand with truth and honor. We both know you don't have any of those things. I should have known you wouldn't follow through with our agreement. Hell, you even hid the fact that you have kids."

"Truth…honor…what would you know about either of those things? We don't have an agreement. You're holding the deed to my land over my head. Furthermore, my kids aren't any of your business."

"If you'll recall, this land belongs to me. I haven't pretended things were anything but what they are. I made you an offer. When you accepted it, I thought you'd at least try to make it work. Furthermore, that acceptance put me smack in the middle of your little family and made the kids my business."

Alex paced to the end of the porch and back. "I don't have a problem with a woman saying no. I've never forced myself on anyone. But tell me, is there any limit to your manipulation and deceit? Is that why the kid's father took off on you? Was he smarter than me? Did he figure out he was being used?"

"I'm not going to discuss my past with you, not when you can't be reasonable." Lacey crossed her arms and turned away. "I've already told you that I never received a single letter from you. If you don't believe that, then you have a problem."

"So you don't deny I wrote to you." Alex felt smug satisfaction until he realized that she really may not have gotten his letters. Damn, this was complicated.

"What's happening between us, Lacey?"

She shook her head. "I don't know. Maybe I was letting a fantasy play out. I don't have much excitement in my life anymore. Being alone with you, the reality crashed down on me and I got scared. It was a stupid thing to do and I'm sorry. Give me a little time to break it to the kids and we'll start packing."

"Dammit, Lacey, I don't want it to end like this." Alex ran his fingers through his hair. He didn't want to act like such a prick to her. He was playing this all wrong. He leaned against the railing to look down at a patch of Mexican heather. "I guess I let my own mind fantasize a little. I thought there might be a chance for us to put the pieces together again."

"You can see now how impossible that is, can't you?" Lacey asked. "You're not ready to be a family man. You'd always resent me for the past. I can't live like that."

"Nobody said it would be easy. There is one thing you have to be honest with me about, though. I have to know about the kids…"

Suddenly a terrible racket stole their attention. Two dogs barked excitedly as they raced back and forth between the porch steps and the east side of the barn. So far, the pigs had barely been noticeable, but now they were squealing loudly. Lacey jumped from the porch and ran toward the pigpen. Alex followed close behind.

Two boards had been broken on the side of the pen. A huge hog's head was pressed through the opening as he tried to escape. A smaller pig streaked across the lawn toward the garden.

Lacey placed her back against the broken boards to

try to hold the larger hog inside. "Get some wood from the pile by the porch. We have to keep the others from getting loose!"

Alex changed direction. In less than a minute he came back with the hammer, box of nails, and two of the stronger boards he'd removed from the porch the week before. He patched the hole in record time, and then stood back to admire his handiwork.

"My garden!" Lacey cried.

The escaped pig was helping himself to a section of turnip greens at the edge of the garden. Alex and Lacey approached him from different directions. The pig ran toward the center of the lawn with the dogs flanking him on either side, biting at his legs. With a surge of speed, Alex caught up to the pig and threw himself down on top of it.

"One of us has to get inside while the other lifts him over," she said.

Alex thought about his expensive sneakers, but Lacey was wearing strappy little sandals that left her feet exposed. He gritted his teeth as he stepped over the side of the pen.

The pig had exhausted himself and was calmer as Lacey picked him up and hefted him into Alex's arms. However, as soon as he realized he was being returned to his prison, the pig proceeded to buck, twist, and scream. Alex was in a fight for his life with a fifty-pound, stinking to high heaven, whirling dervish.

Alex found himself flat on his back in black muck. One large hog snout was pressed to his neck and another to his crotch.

Alex sat up flapping the slime from his arms and yelling for the hogs to get away. Lacey was laughing hysterically.

"I'd give anything for a camera." Lacey could hardly catch her breath. "I'd love for your employees and clients to see you now." The madder Alex looked, the more she laughed. "You're not coming into my house like that, you know."

She walked to the side of the barn, picked up the nozzle of a garden hose and turned it on.

Alex fought through the spray until he could wrap his grimy arms around her in a bear hug.

Minutes later they both lay in the grass, wet and giggling like a couple of kids. Seeing the thin cotton shirt molded against Lacey's curves, his mind went back to when they were kids. She'd looked just like this when she'd come out of the lake: wet, wild, and breathless. His body had the same reaction it did then; raging need, blinding want. The way she gazed at him with half closed eyes, the way she ran the tip of her tongue over her bottom lip, he knew she was feeling it too.

Alex took her breast in his hand, fuller and softer than he remembered. As he lowered his hand to the hem of her white shirt, a streak of grime left a trail. Dammit!

****

Lacey waited for the shower to stop running before she started the washing machine. Alex had told her that he only had a pair of clean boxers and an undershirt left in his bag. He'd need more than that to wear before the kids returned. There'd be no stopping Jerrod from grabbing that twenty-two if he found her alone with Alex in his skivvies. Of course, Jenna would be ready to plan a wedding.

Alex had generously let her shower first. Then she'd chosen a sundress to wear. She was feeling particularly feminine now, probably because she hadn't had male attention in a long time.

It had shocked her when he'd admitted that he hoped they could put the pieces of their former relationship back together. She supposed he'd said it because of her admission that she'd fantasized too. Fantasy was probably a bad choice of words, but that's what had slipped from her lips. At least she hadn't blurted the nature of the other fantasies she'd had during the night. After all, *attention* from a man wasn't the only thing that had been missing from her life.

Would she feel so shy of his advances if she hadn't aged thirteen years and given birth to twins? Probably not, but the last time they'd seen each other she'd been a sweet and innocent seventeen-year-old. Now, gravity was beginning to be her enemy and there were little stretch marks on her body here and there. She still weighed the same, but it had redistributed a little. To put it simply, her size three jeans were only a memory.

It had been so long since she'd felt his touch. His hand on her today had nearly sent her into ecstasy. And then he'd stopped so suddenly. She must not have felt like the girl he'd known before. She had certainly felt the same. No, better, stronger, more sensual, if only for a moment.

She warmed a cup of coffee and a plate of pancakes from breakfast. They were waiting on the table when Alex came in wearing a white T-shirt and a pair of pale blue boxers. Wow! Forget blue jeans vs. business suit, this was his best look yet. Even his feet were sexy, strong and masculine, and yet smooth with nicely trimmed nails.

"Is it okay that I'm barefoot?"

Lacey realized she was still staring at his feet. Since when had she developed a fetish for men's feet?

"Oh, yes, yes they're perfect, I mean it's perfect...ly fine, perfectly fine." Lacey groaned. Could she sound any more like a moron? The wide smile that spread across Alex's face told her, no. When his eyes landed on the plate of food, they widened as well.

"Is this for me, I hope?" Not waiting for an answer, he slid the cup and plate to the other side of the table and sat.

"Is there a reason you need to put your back to the wall?" Lacey asked. "Are we expecting gangsters with machineguns? Are you wanted by the cops? Should I grab my shotgun and keep you covered?"

"It's just a habit." Alex tucked his left hand under the table and picked up his fork with the right.

Lacey watched him eat for a few minutes. She was at a loss for words. His insecurity regarding his scarred arm wasn't necessary. Maybe it was time to point out the elephant in the room. She gathered her courage. "It must be exhausting to always hide your arm that way. Why do you bother? If people can't accept you the way you are, to hell with them."

Alex froze with the last bite of his food halfway to his mouth. He sat his fork down and looked at her with narrowed eyes. Maybe she'd made a mistake.

"Have you ever had a date leave in the middle of dinner because your sleeve drew up? Have you ever had kids whisper behind your back and the only words you could make out were gross, and monster, and Freddy Kruger?"

A hot flush crept up her neck, not from embarrassment, but from anger. Was he accusing her of being like that? He was the one who'd cut their interlude short.

"Women like me don't get asked out on dates. We get plenty of other offers, but not for anything that can be done in public. And yes, people whisper behind my back, but they're not kids. The words I can usually make out are whore, and slut. Oh, I'm sorry, was I supposed to feel sorry for you?"

Alex was shocked. "Is that why you don't go to church with the kids?"

"What do you think?" she answered. "I want my kids to be able to hang out with their friends and be a part of the community without having to hear what the gossips have to say about their mother. For some reason, it's only a problem when I'm there."

Alex wondered if that was true, or if that's what the kids led her to believe. One thing he was certain of, no one would talk about her like that in his presence. He took her hand. "Those are just a few small minded old biddies. No one that matters would say something like that about you."

"Oh really? Does that include your mother?" Lacey jerked her hand away. "Why do you think I didn't get your address from her all those years ago? She wouldn't give it to me. She said you were better off not hearing from me. She wanted you to find a nice, decent girl, someone she could be proud to have in her family."

"That's not true," Alex insisted.

"Don't take my word for it." Lacey stood and went to the sink to run dishwater. "Ask her yourself."

****

Alex watched Lacey as she kept her back to him. He felt like he'd been slapped. How had things gone so wrong so fast? They'd practically made love on the back lawn a few minutes ago, and now, she'd thrown this bit of news at him. It had to have been a misunderstanding. His mother and hers had been friends since high school. They'd attended backyard barbeques and birthday parties for each other. They played bridge together for heaven's sake.

His relationship with his mom had always been close. She'd never said anything off color about Lacey. At least, not that he'd ever heard. She could be a little tough on people sometimes, but not mean.

Could that misunderstanding have been the catalyst that had thrown her into another man's arms? God, he hoped not.

He'd never understand women if he lived to be a hundred.

Alex brought his empty dishes to the sink. Then he transferred his wet clothes into the dryer. If it wasn't for the promise he'd made to help Jerrod, he'd leave when he had clothes to wear. But his clothes wouldn't be ready for almost hour and Jerrod would be home shortly thereafter.

After the last dish was washed, Lacey stepped out to the front porch. Alex followed to try and smooth things over. These were the times that made a grown man feel like a helpless little girl.

When he left the kitchen and walked into the living room, he saw her through the front screen door. The sun shone on her light auburn hair as she sat on the porch steps. Damn, she looked delicate in that little yellow sundress. He never used the word delicate, it wasn't masculine. But he couldn't think of any other word to describe her as she sat with her knees pulled up to her chest and nothing on her shoulders but two little bows.

Both the dogs who had helped them with the runaway pig were cuddled against her. He almost felt jealous of the affection they were receiving, but they'd earned it. That stupid pig would still be running them ragged if the dogs hadn't chased him down.

"Those are a couple of beautiful dogs. Have you had them long?"

Lacey turned to look up at him through the screen. Her eyes were rimmed red and her lashes were damp. Her nose was hot pink and her lips were swollen. She'd been crying. He never could stand to see her cry.

She swiped the inside of her wrist over her eyes and sniffed. "Five years. Ever since they were weaned. They're names are Buck and Bella. They're part of the family. Come out and say hello. They've been curious about you."

Alex joined her on the top step. The female Border collie stayed against Lacey's side. The male moved off the steps and sat on the ground, as still as a statue in front of him. He eyed Alex suspiciously. Were all the males on this farm going to give him a hard time?

"I forgot you had dogs until they showed up this morning. I hadn't heard a single bark before that. Where've they been?"

"Working of course," Lacey replied. "They usually stay with the cattle. You being here made them a little off their game, and then the pigpen escape made them more nervous. They'll be fine after a little loving."

Alex wanted to tell her that he could do with a little

loving, but he held his tongue. Her nerves were still too raw. "You were serious about everyone working for their supper."

"Buck and Bella are the best herders in the county," Lacey bragged. "They've won several ribbons for their skill with cattle."

"No kidding?" Alex held out his flat hand. Bella came around to sniff it, but Buck just blew out a huff.

Lacey stood up and brushed the dust and dog hair from her skirt. "I guess I'd better get started on my chores."

Bella walked down the steps and toward the side of the house. Buck remained in place staring at Alex.

"I'll help," Alex offered as he stood to follow Lacey inside. If that dog could handle a small herd of cattle without supervision, he didn't want to be alone with him. Not until he had a change of attitude.

Yeah, you'd better," Lacey laughed, "before someone sees you outside in your underwear."

In the kitchen, Lacey pulled a bowl of diced potatoes from the refrigerator and drained off the water. Next, she began peeling boiled eggs. Now here was something Alex knew about, potato salad. He drained a portion of relish to add, along with a huge dollop of mayonnaise, and a spoonful of mustard.

"Lacey, maybe we should talk about the wedding plans before the kids get home. They definitely put a new spin on the situation, especially Jerrod. I see now that it may take more than a month to work this out."

"I absolutely agree," Lacey said.

Alex wondered if she really did. The smile she wore looked less than genuine.

"As a matter of fact, I've been thinking about the

cutest Victorian house on the corner of Main Street and Osceola Lane. It's near the school. The kids would be able to walk every day. It's only a little smaller than this one and has a fenced back yard for Buck and Bella. I'd be able to find a job in town. The only work I've ever done has been this farm, but I've always kept good books. I should be able to do the same for another type business. Once they finish putting on the new roof on that house, it'll be ready to rent. I figure I could move into it before the end of the month. I can't imagine what it would be like to have free time."

Alex was surprised by how much thought she'd put into this. "Is that really what you want? Are you ready to give up so easily? You'd be willing to walk away from this farm after all the work you've put into it? You'd be ready to give up on me after just finding each other again? I understand that you don't want to marry me. You made that clear thirteen years ago, but what about the friendship we had growing up? Doesn't that mean anything?"

"Of course it does." Lacey wiped her hands on a dishcloth that had been covering a glass bowl. Then she rolled a fluffy ball of dough out of the bowl and onto a floured board. "I've learned to be independent. That means doing whatever I have to, to make ends meet. I can't borrow the money to buy this farm. I have to give it up. No hard feelings. Business is business. I respect that. We can still be friends."

Alex couldn't help but admire her strength and resolve. Why couldn't her cantankerous old grandfather see her worth and help her? The Double J was who she was. She needed this farm, but she also needed her dignity.

"Maybe something could be worked out," he said. "Let me take your books home to look them over. I'd like to think this over and talk to you about it next weekend. I could come back again next Friday evening, if that's okay with you." Alex riffled through the spices until he found paprika, parsley, garlic powder, and white pepper.

"Wait a minute," Lacey exclaimed. "I'm making that salad with your mother's recipe. I thought you'd like it that way."

Alex shrugged. "She never mentions that my dad adds his own ingredients. My mom is not the great cook she pretends to be, but Dad covers for her. Trust me. You'll like it better this way."

If he couldn't charm her out of her panties, he'd at least impress her with his cooking.

Chapter Ten

Alex slammed the tailgate after the supplies had been loaded. He hoped they had everything they needed. Jerrod had gathered five fence posts, three spools of wire, two large bags of cement, a couple of empty plastic feed containers, a posthole digger, a shovel, and an old wooden box with assorted hand tools. It felt weird to let someone else take the lead, especially a kid, and most especially when the kid was Jerrod. The boy wasn't old enough to have a hair on his ass, but he had a ton of bad attitude.

Alex's T-shirt and the bandana around his head were already soaked with sweat. It had been a long time since he'd done anything outdoors besides running a park trail or overseeing a development project. He hoped to make it back to Orlando before his muscles locked up. The last thing he wanted to do was wuss-out in front of Lacey, or even worse, Jerrod.

As soon as the boy came back with the truck keys, they'd be on their own. He didn't have a clue what he'd talk about with Jerrod. He didn't know a single thing about kids.

Leaning against the fender, he watched Lacey lead a chestnut mare from the barn. She looked so damned sexy in that yellow sundress, old cowboy boots, and beat-up cowboy hat. She was all woman with a little bit of a dirty side. She was fearless. He couldn't imagine her backing down from any challenge. Yes, she'd lost the blush of youth, but it had been replaced by a fiery passion. Alex figured it was a good tradeoff. He just had to find a way to tap into some of that passion.

"Are we gonna get to work, or do you plan to stay here and drool over my mom for a while longer?"

Alex snatched the keys from Jerrod's hand. "I'm not drooling, I'm admiring. When you get older you'll understand the difference." Jerrod's age and size were his sore spots and couldn't resist getting in a dig.

"We're wasting daylight. If we don't get that fence fixed this weekend, we'll start losing cattle. Of course, the bind that would put Mom in would make it easier for you to take this place away from her, wouldn't it?"

They slid into the truck seat and slammed their doors. Around Lacey, Jerrod seemed to be cooling his attitude, but obviously, that was just for her benefit. Alex decided to try a little psychology.

He headed to the west side of the property. It wasn't hard to find the part of the fence that needed repair. Already there were three cows hanging around, thinking about the grass on the other side. A couple beeps of the horn changed their minds and they lumbered away.

"Okay, Jerrod, where do you want me to start?"

Jerrod's brows drew together. "What do you mean?"

"Well, it's your fence and your job." Alex stepped out into the grassy pasture. "I guess that puts you in charge."

As they walked to the back of the truck, Alex could have sworn that Jerrod was walking a little taller.

"You can use a set of side-cutters to snip the bad

wire off where it's still attached. Be careful that it doesn't snap back at you. And leave enough tail to wrap around the post." Jerrod puffed his chest out. "I've got five posts to replace in this section. I've been sinking the new ones in cement. I just about have them all replaced now."

That would definitely make the fence stronger. He had to admire the kid's ingenuity.

As fast as he could cut the wire, Jerrod had the ends wrapped and stapled down. When the five rotted posts were bare, Alex dug them out while Jerrod unloaded the new ones. Each hole was made larger to accommodate its share of cement mixed with water from a nearby trough. When the posts were set, they took a break to allow the cement to set.

"Got anything to drink in this cooler?" Alex started toward the bed of the truck.

Jerrod ran to reach the truck ahead of him. "Umm, I think I forgot to bring anything." He seemed as nervous as a mouse in a lion cage.

Something was up. What could the boy be hiding? He reached over Jerrod's shoulder and flipped the top up on the cooler. Inside was a six-pack of sodas along with a few bottles of water.

"Are you gonna tell my mom?"

Alex helped himself to one of the cans. "Your mom must be pretty strict. What would happen if I did tell her?"

"No dessert for a month, I bet." Jerrod kicked a clump of dirt. "She worries about us eating healthy and all that. She worries about everything. I can't blame her. It's not easy being a single mom. But dang it, sometimes it's hard to follow all those rules."

Alex handed Jerrod a can of soda. "It'll be our secret then. Besides that, you've earned it. You work hard, and you're stronger than I expected."

"You mean, because I'm so small," Jerrod groused.

"I don't know much about kids, but you don't seem all that small to me."

Jerrod sat on the edge of the tailgate. "All the guys at school call me Shorty and Runt and stuff like that. They're just joking, but it's embarrassing when girls are around. I'm the smallest guy in my class."

"I remember those days." Alex sat next to Jerrod. "Your mom can tell you how small I was as a kid. It seemed like I had a target on my back for every bully in school. I was always the last one picked for a team. My friends made jokes about it too. And yes, it was embarrassing around the girls. It caused me to have a big chip on my shoulder for a while."

"I think you're just making that up to make me feel better." Jerrod sneered. "I looked at mom's yearbooks last night in my room. You were a big football star in high school. They must've had a hundred pictures of you in there."

"So you were checking me out," Alex laughed. "I didn't know you were such a good detective. It's true that I was big by then. I hit a growth spurt that lasted all the way through middle school. My mom thought it would never stop. She complained all the time about how fast I outgrew my clothes and shoes. By the end of tenth grade I was as tall as I am now. It took a few more years and a lot of hard work to fill out though."

"Really? You're not bullshitting me are you?" Jerrod was awe struck. "How old were you when you got as big as the other guys?"

"I guess it was in about eighth grade." Alex was glad to give the kid a little hope. "By the time I started high school, I was passing half of them up."

"We'd better get back to work," Jerrod walked to the truck door and reached under the seat. He pulled out a pair of work gloves and tossed them to Alex. "You may need these."

"You couldn't have found those a couple of hours ago?"

"Sorry." Jerrod grinned. "I just remembered they were there."

Replacing the section of fence had been hard work. Alex couldn't believe that Lacey and two children had been doing this kind of thing on their own. That was going to change. And now was as good a time as any to get Jerrod used to the idea. He picked up an old post and threw it into the back of the truck while Jerrod gathered the tools. "These posts and the old wood from the porch would make a good bonfire. Maybe I should pick up some hotdogs and marshmallows before I come back next weekend. Do you think Jenna and your mom would like that?"

"Maybe," Jerrod mumbled.

Alex tried to think of what to say next. His gut told him that Jerrod's attitude was taking a southern turn. The old truck slowly bounced and creaked back toward the house.

Finally, Jerrod broke the silence. "Are you planning on coming around a lot, Mr. Benson?"

"Maybe. Are you asking what my intentions are, Jerrod?"

"I guess I am."

Alex brought the truck to a stop and shut off the

engine. He turned to look Jerrod in the eye. The defiant look was back on the boy's face, he was losing ground again. Damn, this kid was tough.

"Jerrod, you know I've known your mom since she was just a baby. What you don't know is that we were really close at one time. It was a long time ago, when we were barely more than kids ourselves. A lot has happened to both of us since then, one thing being you and your sister. There are still a few things we'll have to work out. But now that I've found her again, I realized I still have feelings for her. I think she may come around to feeling the same. I want to get to know you and Jenna, and hopefully, someday, make you part of my life. It would be a lot easier if you could work with me on this."

"Maybe." Jerrod paused. "So, what you're saying is, you're thinking of making me a redheaded stepchild, for real." He swallowed hard and looked out the passenger window. "Did she ever tell you about our dad?"

Jerrod seemed sullen. He'd made a mistake by being so up-front about his intentions so soon. It was too late to turn back now, though. "Jenna said your mom doesn't like to talk about him. She also told me that he doesn't know about the two of you and that he's never been around."

"Mom said if he did know about us, he'd love us."

"Jenna told me that too." The despair radiated from the boy. All he could offer for comfort were words. "I imagine he'd be damn proud to have two great kids like you and Jenna, but don't you think your mom deserves to be loved too?"

Jerrod turned toward Alex. Tears had collected in

his green eyes, but he held his chin out the way Lacey did when she was being stubborn.

"Jenna probably didn't tell you the rest of what Mom said. She said she'd loved our dad more than she ever loved anyone. She said she'd never love like that again. Will it be okay with you to take second place, Mr. Benson?"

Alex tried to keep the emotion from showing in his expression as they stared at each other. He didn't want Jerrod to know he'd just delivered the most painful blow he'd ever felt.

"You know, someday you and Jenna will be grown and on your own. Your mom will be all alone. Is that what you want for her?"

"My dad will be back by then. I'm going to find him and tell him everything."

"How do you plan to do that, kid?"

"Granddad knows who my dad is. I can tell by some of the things I've heard him say to my mom. He doesn't seem to like him much." Jerrod gave him an angry glare. "But when I get a little older, he'll tell me who he is. Then, I'll go find him and bring him back. That's what I've planned to do for a long time now. My mom will be happy then, just you wait and see. If she married you it would just be in order to keep the farm. That's all you mean to her. This farm isn't worth that much."

"Good luck with that, kid." Alex knew Jarrod hated being called kid. He was just being an ass because the boy had gotten the best of him. He straightened in his seat and started the truck's engine again. "The sun's going down. We'd better get back."

Chapter Eleven

Lacey stepped out to the front porch when she heard the old truck approaching. Jerrod and Alex both looked tired and dirty as they came up the steps.

"Come in and let me get you something to drink while you get cleaned up."

"I'm just going to grab my things and head home." Alex followed her as far as the other side of the screen door. "It's getting late. I've already stayed longer then I'd planned. I'll take a shower at home and fall straight into bed. Morning comes awfully early you know. I have a meeting at the top of my schedule."

Something had changed about Alex, but she couldn't put her finger on what it was. Maybe he'd gotten more hard work and hot sun then he was used to, this weekend.

On the other hand, Jerrod looked downright chipper. He walked up to Alex and offered his hand. "It was nice meeting you, Mr. Benson. You did a great job on that fence today."

"You too, Jerrod. I wouldn't mind if you call me Alex." He shook the boy's hand. "I meant what I said. You really are a hard worker. Your mom's lucky to have a guy like you around."

"We get by," Jerrod said. "You have a safe trip home, Alex. Maybe we'll see you again sometime."

Lacey watched her son walk up the stairs, then

turned to Alex. Something had definitely changed. Why hadn't he said anything to Jerrod about coming back next weekend?

"I hope you didn't have any trouble with Jerrod today," she said.

"No. I seriously meant what I said. He works as hard as any man I know, and he's nearly as strong. You've done a damned good job raising him." Alex still watched the top of the stairs, although Jerrod had disappeared from sight. Was he reluctant to make eye contact? "We talked about a lot of things and got to know each other a little. One thing I learned is that he loves you very much."

Alex picked up his gym bag and strap it over his shoulder. His words were polite, but his tense jaw said that he could easily rip a tree out of the ground with his bare hands.

"You're not leaving so soon, are you, Mr. Benson?" Jenna bounded into the living room with her usual exuberance.

"Not without saying goodbye to you doll-face." His face lit up at the sight of his biggest admirer. "You have to call me Alex, though. I can't deal with being called by my father's name. He's so old."

"I wish you could stay," Jenna sighed. "You're so much fun."

"I wish I could too, honey." A *but* seemed to hang in the air. What more did he want to say? This was killing Lacey.

"Mom and I put a care package together for you." Jenna was already heading to the kitchen, speaking over her shoulder. "I'll put it in your car so you won't forget it."

"This has been the greatest weekend I've had in a long time." Alex tucked a piece of hair behind Lacey's ear. "And that reminds me, I want you to keep an eye on my pig. I've decided that, since he cost me a good pair of shoes, I'm claiming him for my own. From now on, his name is Harry, for Harry Houdini."

"You're welcome to visit him anytime you like." Lacey forced a smile. "I have to warn you, though, one day you may be eating him for supper."

Alex placed his hands at her waist. "Kiss me goodbye, you heartless woman."

Why fight it? She wanted that kiss. As she sank into his warm gentle arms, Lacey knew she wasn't heartless. Right then, her heart was aching for a lot more than a mere kiss, even more than mere sex. She wanted his heart.

She smiled and waved from the front porch as his car turned onto the road. A moment later, Jerrod came up behind her. He was only wearing a pair of shorts and his hair was still wet from his shower.

"What did you and Alex find to talk about all afternoon?" she asked.

"We talked about a lot of stuff. You know, guy stuff. Stuff you can't really talk about with your mom." Jerrod shrugged. "Anyway, Alex was pretty cool. He let me be the boss and everything. I'm going to go up to my room and get some reading done. I've still got a few books on my summer reading list, and the one I'm on now isn't horrible."

After he went back inside, Lacey realized he hadn't asked for anything to eat. He hadn't mentioned food at all. Something was definitely wrong.

****

Alex had only driven five miles from the Double J when he pulled onto a path toward the water. It was more overgrown then it had been thirteen years ago. He knew there was a risk of scratching the paint on his BMW, but he didn't give a damn. He reached a small clearing that was surrounded by oaks so big and thick that they canopied the whole area and only let in a few rays of sunlight. Approximately three yards on the other side of the trees was the lake, but this spot was well hidden from view.

He wondered when Lacey had last been here. Did she ever think about this place?

The first time he'd come was the evening he followed Lacey, after her parents' funerals. It was so dark he'd had to build a small fire. She'd been crying because of the things Mrs. Dell said to her, and of course because her parents weren't there to support her and make everything okay again.

He'd held her for a long time, and then he made love to her for the first time. He'd been too young to realize how vulnerable she was at that moment. All he knew was that he wanted her. He had for a long time.

They'd fumbled through the act, her being a virgin and him feeling like one. But it had been beautiful. Afterward, they met there nearly every day for a month. They made love, and then lay in the grass naked, wrapped in each other's arms and talking until they fell asleep.

They sat under the tree where their names were carved when he told her his plan to postpone college and join the Navy. She'd cried then too. He'd felt terrible, but he'd thought he was doing the responsible, grown-up thing. She promised to write as often as she could. He promised to come back for her. Then it was over. Neither promise had been kept.

Now fate had just fed him a big shit sandwich. It had teased him with a glimpse of the woman she'd become and of all he'd missed. But there was no way to turn back the clock. There was no way to remove the scars on his body or his soul. And, no way to erase her love for another man. He'd lost…again.

Why had he pushed his way back into her life? Why had he allowed himself to fall in love with her a second time? Yeah, he had to admit he loved her. He supposed he'd never really stopped. But it was harder now. There were a lot more complications.

Everything that could have gone wrong had, and still, he'd had the time of his life. He'd let his guard down.

While one of her kids worshipped him and fed his ego, the other tore him down and put him in his place, which was no place in their lives. Now, he would have to walk away again.

He should have stayed away from her. He shouldn't have come back to Florida. He sure as hell shouldn't have bought property in Indian Lakes. What had he been thinking?

When Alex looked down to put his shifter in Reverse, he noticed the box in the passenger seat. On the lid was a smiley face with its tongue sticking out on one side and one curlicue on the top of its head— Jenna's artwork, no doubt.

Alex couldn't resist opening the box to see what kind of care package they'd made for him. On the top were two thick ledger books. Their covers were marked in bold print with Lacey's brand, overlapping J's that sat at an angle. The first showed the previous year and the other, the year before that. He'd forgotten he'd asked to look them over.

Under the books were plastic containers of cold fried chicken, potato salad, green beans, homemade rolls, and a generous slice of pie. A lump formed in Alex's throat. Leaving all three of them was going to hurt like hell. Yes, despite Jerrod's surly disposition, he'd miss him too. How had they all gotten under his skin so quickly?

Chapter Twelve

The kids hadn't been this quiet at the supper table since the last time they were in trouble. Lacey couldn't think of a reason for it today. The last four days had gone by without incident. Everyone had done their chores and gotten along. It had almost been *too* perfect.

Jenna seemed her usual self most of the time. She'd probably just run out of things to say about Alex. He'd been her main topic of conversation since he'd left on Sunday evening.

"You seem awfully quiet tonight, Jenna. Is something on your mind?"

"Well, yes." Jenna set her fork down and knit her brow. "Granddad came by this morning with two flats of strawberries. He wants us to make some jam. You were in the corral exercising Ms. Begley's mare so I put them in the outside cooler. I figure I'll get started on them in the morning."

"We make jam for him every summer. It shouldn't be a problem." Jenna still looked concerned about something. Lacey knew there'd been more to her grandfather's visit. "Did he have anything else to say?"

Jenna took a deep breath before she replied. "Jerrod and I have always ridden in the Heritage Day Parade with granddad. He says he's tired of driving that old Model-T for the bank. He says it looks like the bank is showing off both their old relics. He thinks the new bank president should take it over."

Lacey put effort into keeping a straight face. It was a good thing Jenna had taken that deep breath, otherwise, she might have passed out from the long tirade. "Now, if that's the way Granddad feels about it, I think we should respect his wishes."

"Oh, I do," Jenna interrupted. "That's not what I was thinking about."

"Well, if it isn't the strawberry jam or the Model-T, what is eating at you?" Jenna could wear a person out before she got to the point.

"I'm thinking about riding Buttercup in the parade." Her face lit up. "Maybe Jerrod could ride Drifter. We could put their blue ribbons on their harnesses or saddles so everyone could see that they're champions. It might even bring in more business."

How could she tell Jenna that they may not have a business by then? Without the farm, Buttercup and Drifter would have to be sold along with her own horse, Stardust. Jenna was so excited about the idea; the reality would be like a slap in the face.

"Let me think about it."

"What do you think, Jerrod?" Jenna was looking for reinforcements.

"Huh?" Jerrod looked up with a blank stare. "What are y'all talking about?"

If Lacey hadn't known better she'd think Jerrod had just woken up. Was he sick? Had he been outside in the heat for too long? Something had been eating at her boy all week and it was starting to take a toll on him.

"Jenna, would you finish up outside. Jerrod can help me with the dishes."

"Okay, Mom." Jenna bounded out the door,

energized by her new plans.

Jerrod began stacking the plates on the table. His meal was only half-eaten, but he prepared to add the remainder to the slop bucket. He hadn't had a good appetite all week. For a boy his age, this was serious.

"Are you feeling okay, son? You've hardly been eating lately."

"It's just been hot is all. I'm okay."

Lacey took him by the shoulders and turned him around. There were blue shadows under his eyes. He hadn't been sleeping well, either. Considering the amount of work he'd been catching up, this was also serious. A body that worked so hard could get awfully run down if it wasn't properly taken care of.

"What's going on with you? You haven't been yourself for days. If something is bothering you, I want to know. There isn't anything we can't work out if you're honest with me."

"Jeez, Mom, you make it sound like I'm on drugs or something." Jerrod scowled. "I've just had a lot on my mind."

A chill ran down Lacey's spine at the mention of drugs. Other parents she knew were battling that problem. She hoped she'd never see that day. "You haven't been yourself since Alex Benson came to visit. Did something happen when the two of you went out to mend the fence? Did he say or do something to upset you?"

"No, Mom," Jerrod turned his eyes away. "Everything is fine."

"I have Alex's phone number. Maybe I should ask him." Lacey let go of Jerrod's shoulders. "I want this straightened out before he comes back."

"Oh that would be really great. Make him think I'm some kind of a baby. He's the only one around here who doesn't already." Jerrod flopped back into his chair at the table.

"Is this about something I've done?" Lacey asked. "I know you're growing up, and sometimes I don't know how to handle it."

"You don't seem to have so much trouble handling it with Jenna." Jerrod folded his arms and looked away.

"Jenna's a girl," Lacey reminded him. "Believe it or not, I was a girl at one time. I know how she thinks and what she's feeling. It's altogether different with a boy. I've never been around boys all that much. I thought it would be good for you to have a man to talk to. Jerrod, you have to help me understand what's going on."

"Well," Jerrod began. "It was good talking to Alex. He's an okay guy. We talked about serious man stuff, you know? It got me thinking about the future a little. Mom, do you ever think about the future and what it'll be like when Jenna and me are all grown up?"

Lacey smiled. He was finally opening up a little. Now wasn't the time to start correcting his grammar. "I think about it all the time. I've been putting away money for college since the two of you were born. You're both so smart I want you to have the opportunity to be whatever you'd like. Then, I hope you'll find love and settle down. Mostly, I want you to be happy."

"What about you?" Jerrod asked. "What will you do then?"

"I'll be fine." Lacey reached across the table and took his hand. His hands were so much bigger than they used to be. They were calloused and scarred by hard work. He was becoming a man, not someday, but soon. "Maybe you guys will live close by so that I can visit you often."

"What about love, Mom? Don't you ever think about having someone to love?"

"I'll always have you and Jenna. Someday I hope to have a few grandchildren too. That's more love than any woman could hope for."

Jerrod gave her a stern look. "You know that's not what I meant. Stop treating me like a little kid."

This time, Lacey was the one to turn away. "Exactly what are you getting at?"

"I want to know if you still love my father as much as you used to."

The abrupt question almost made Lacey gasp. She tried to hedge around the subject. "I know this conversation is way overdue. And, I do want to answer all your questions. I promise I will soon, but I need a little more time."

"I just need a yes or no, Mom." Jerrod's voice was lower than she'd ever heard it. "That's all I need to know right now."

"The answer is yes," Lacey whispered. "I still love him just as much."

Jerrod squeezed her hand. "Thanks. I didn't mean to give you a hard time. You know how much I love you. I don't even mind doing these dishes by myself if you'd like to soak in the tub for a while tonight."

Lacey gave her son a big hug before she went to her room. She sat on her big empty bed and wished she had someone to cuddle up to, someone she could share her thoughts with. She wished that person could be

Alex.

The chances of that happening got slimmer with every day that passed without a phone call. She hadn't heard a word from him since he'd left on Sunday.

Would he be back this weekend, or had he walked away again? There was only one way to find out.

Lacey took the business card out of her nightstand and looked at it. A. J. Benson, he didn't even use his given name anymore, at least not in his world. Everything had changed about him except the way he made her feel. He made her feel alive again, full of promise and passion.

She picked up the phone next to her bed and dialed his cell phone number. She didn't know where he might be at this time of the evening. A recording came through the receiver. "All circuits are busy at this time. Please try your call again later."

She hung up. It wasn't unusual for the lines to be busy at the end of the workday. Then she remembered what Alex had said before. He didn't leave work until after dark. She dialed his office number.

"Thank you for calling East Coast Land Development," his assistant's voice said on a recorded message. "Our Orlando headquarters is closed, due to relocation. All current clients will be contacted within the coming week. If your call is urgent, please contact the satellite office nearest you. As always, East Coast Land Development is glad to assist in your future growth."

Lacey's hand felt numb as she placed the receiver back into the cradle. What did that mean? Alex hadn't said a word about relocating. Was his office moving to another building in Orlando, another city, another state?

Why hadn't he said anything? Why hadn't he called? Was this the reason for his odd behavior Sunday?

Lacey realized that her breaths were short and shallow. The room seemed to be swaying. She was close to hyperventilating. She bent over and took a few deep breaths until she regained control. Then she picked up the phone again and dialed the number he'd written on the back of the card, his home number. The message on that line confirmed her fears. The number had been disconnected. He was gone.

Chapter Thirteen

Alex gazed into the bathroom mirror. Even with a shower and shave he looked like hell warmed over. There were blue shadows under his eyes from lack of sleep. His face looked gaunt after missing most of his meals this past week. He packed his shave kit and slid it into his gym bag. Everything else had already been packed and stacked in the living room for the movers to pick up in the morning.

He collected the dirty clothes from the floor, embarrassed to realize he'd worn the same T-shirt and shorts for the last three days. There didn't seem to be any reason to change. He'd stayed at home to pack and make all arrangements by phone. He wadded the clothes into a ball and stuffed them into the trash bin.

What to do with one wet towel? It was one he'd brought home from the gym wrapped around an ice bag after he'd been hit in the head by a racquetball. He dropped it into the trash along with the clothes.

On his way through the bedroom, he noticed the empty wire hangers from the cleaners in the open closet. They were the only sign that anyone had ever stepped foot in the room. Alex realized that no one had been in this room besides himself. He had an oak tallboy in the corner and a matching nightstand by the full-sized bed. The only other color in the room had been a green blanket that covered his white sheets and pillows, now packed away. He had helped Lacey change the sheets on the beds at the farm. Each room was decorated in bright colors and demonstrated the personality of the person who lived in that room.

In the living room, his expensive leather sofa and chairs were pushed together in the center of the floor. The marble-topped side tables were upended on top of the matching coffee table. Lacey's furniture was old and faded, but a man could sink into it and feel at home. It was furniture that had watched old movies late at night and supported babies as they pulled up to stand on shaky little legs. It might not have a lot of style, but it had history, family history.

The painting that leaned against the wall in the foyer had cost a small fortune. He'd trade it any day for the school pictures of silly toothless smiles that adorned Lacey's stairwell.

Boxes and packing paper littered the top of his chrome and glass dining table. The tall-backed, brocade chairs were lined up against the wall. It made him think about a catfish supper that covered Lacey's old wooden table with mismatched chairs.

His kitchen was empty now. The glossy white cabinets and stainless steel appliances had hardly been used. He closed his eyes and imagined the delicious aroma of fresh apples combined with sweet onions and coffee, Lacey's kitchen.

There was a gnawing in Alex's stomach and a heavy feeling in his chest. It was a feeling he recalled from long ago, when he'd left for the Navy. He was homesick, homesick for that rundown little farm house.

Jerrod was his biggest obstacle. How could he make him accept a man in his life, other than the one that had abandoned him before he was born? And, would Lacey ever forgive him for the sins she felt he'd committed thirteen years ago.

A tap sounded on Alex's front door.

Mary Ann stood in the hallway with a sad smile. "I'm sure going to miss you, boss."

"Are you positive you can't come with me?" Alex asked.

Mary Ann shook her head. "I can't ask the kids to leave their schools. Brian just made the varsity team. Besides that, I'm looking forward to running my own satellite office. We'll probably be in touch more than you think."

Alex picked up his gym bag and handed over his apartment keys. "Thanks for taking care of the movers for me."

"No problem."

He placed a brotherly kiss on her cheek. "Take care of yourself, kiddo."

"You too, boss."

****

Lacey walked back to the feed store with three full bags from the *Shop-a-rama*. She was as self-sustaining as possible, but there were some things that were impossible to grow, such as laundry detergent, soap, and toilet tissue.

The fall seeds and fertilizer had been loaded into the back of her pickup and she'd placed an order of feed and hay to be delivered.

Mr. Hanover owned the feed store, as well as the house on Osceola that she'd told Alex about. When she saw him step outside to light his pipe, she decided it was a good time to ask about renting the house. Perhaps she'd also ask about a job. Before she could put her bags inside the truck, she dropped her keys in the gravel parking lot.

"Let me get those for you." Mr. Hanover ambled toward her. "You shouldn't be carrying all this stuff by yourself. Where are those two scallywags of yours?"

"I dropped them off at the skate park. Sometimes it's easier to do things myself then have the kids underfoot."

"My Martha used to say the same thing," Hanover chuckled. "Now it would be nice to get a visit from them more than once a year. Cherish the time you have with those kids. It passes by too quickly."

Lacey nodded. She couldn't think of a way to ease into the subject so she just dove straight in. "I noticed you put a new roof on your rental house. How soon do you think you'll be ready to rent it?"

"Never." Hanover chuckled again. "It's the damnedest thing. I got an offer to sell the house on Monday. It was a generous deal. Now, here it is, Friday, and we closed on the house this morning."

Lacey was stunned. "That was extremely fast."

"It sure was," he agreed. "I guess it pays to deal with a big real estate outfit. That Benson boy knows how to get things done."

"Benson?" No, it couldn't be. Alex wouldn't do this to her.

"Yep, that younger Benson boy is back in town. He's a big shot real estate man now." Hanover rambled on, not realizing Lacey was nearly in shock. "He was telling me that he'd bought some other property around here and he hadn't decided what to do with it yet. Anyhow, he wanted a place in town. I guess someone had told him about the old Victorian. He said the location was perfect for his needs."

"Just what did he say his needs are?" Lacey cringed at the trace of indignation in her voice.

"He didn't really say." Hanover shrugged. "All I know is that I made enough money to take Martha on a vacation to see the grandkids. That's all she's talked about since the last one was born."

"Mr. Hanover," a young male clerk leaned out the door of the store and called, "you're needed on the phone, sir."

"I'll be glad to hand this place over to my manager for a couple of weeks." Hanover grumbled as he walked away.

Lacey took a few minutes to calm her heart rate before she headed to Osceola Lane. She was going to give Alex Benson a piece of her mind.

She parked her old truck in the side yard next to his fancy silver BMW. A moving van was unloading in the driveway. A large wooden sign leaned against the front porch with the words East Coast Land Development printed under a silhouette of a sprawling tree. The front door stood open.

In the living room, one wall was covered in four drawer, black filing cabinets. To the left was an oak desk and black leather secretary chair. Two matching guest chairs faced it. At the right were the sofa, chairs, and tables she and Alex had used in his Orlando office.

Through the arched doorway she could see into the formal dining room that now contained his huge mahogany desk and the chairs that went with it. His credenza fit perfectly under the bay windows.

The kitchen door swung open and Jenna walked

through with a pitcher of iced tea in one hand and a stack of disposable cups in the other. Lacey's heart sank. Her own daughter was aiding the enemy.

"What in the world are you doing here?"

Two men passed carrying a brown leather sofa toward the stairs. The one walking backward almost ran into her.

"Hey, kid, are you sure he wants this stuff in the front bedroom up there?" one of the men asked.

"Yes," Jenna answered. "The largest room will be the sitting room."

She turned back to her mother. "Isn't it great Mom? Alex is going to be working here and living right upstairs, all but the kitchen, that is. It would be kind of hard to move that. But we'll get to see him all the time now."

"I never gave you permission to leave the park. What are you doing here?" Lacey asked again.

"We saw Alex's car drive by with a moving truck behind it. We decided to follow on our skateboards, just for a little way. We didn't have any idea he was moving into Mr. Hanover's old house."

Alex said he'd like to take us all out for supper after the movers leave. You were included in the invitation too, of course. He says he owes you one for last weekend. I was supposed to go ask you, but I wanted to make this tea first."

At the top of the stairs, one of the movers dropped the end of the sofa and cursed. Lacey looked up and saw that Alex was standing on the landing looking down at her.

Why did he have to be wearing low riding jeans and a loose, long sleeved shirt, completely unbuttoned?

Sweat coated his washboard abs and rock hard chest. The spread of silky hair on his chest glistened teasingly. His hair had sprung into its natural state of ringlets. To top it all off, he was barefoot. Her heart reached top speed and she was melting into a warm puddle of need. Only Alex had ever had the ability to reduce her to this state.

She quickly looked back at her daughter. "No, I'm afraid not, Jenna. I already have plans for supper at home."

"Pour me a cup of that tea, Jen."

Lacey was surprised to hear Jerrod's voice behind her. She turned to find him carrying a couple of cardboard boxes marked *bathroom stuff.*

"For heaven's sake," she exclaimed. "What are you doing?"

"I figured I'd help out," Jerrod answered. "After all, Alex helped me last weekend."

"You have enough work to do at home." Between her kids jumping ship and Alex looking sexier than homemade sin as he took them aboard, Lacey was on her last nerve. "Both of you need to put these things down and get into the truck. It's time to leave."

"But Mom," Jenna whined. "Alex said I can help him arrange the furniture. I'm going to help him decorate this place, new curtains and pictures and all."

Alex descended the stairs with the movements of a cat. Dear God, don't let him touch her or her clothes would surely fall off.

"You'd better do as your mom says, kids." Why did he have to look so good? "There's no way we'll get all this done in one day, anyway. Thanks for the help. I'll see you soon."

Lacey silently stared into Alex's eyes as she waited for the kids to be out of hearing distance. She could feel the nerves jumping under her skin. It took every bit of willpower she had not to reach up and slap his face or kiss him to death. She didn't know which urge was stronger.

"I know I should have asked before I let them stay. I'm sorry."

"Why? You knew I was hoping to get this house. You know that a rental rarely comes available in a town this size. Why did you have to take it?"

"You were right. This house is nice and it's in a great location."

"What are the kids and I supposed to do now, live in our truck?" The pitch of her voice had gone high and whiny, which only annoyed her more.

"You still have the farm."

"No, you have the farm, remember? You bought it out from under me."

Alex placed his hands on her shoulders. "I've looked at your books. You really know how to make the Double J work. It's who you are. You don't want to give it up."

"You and I both know I can't buy it from you." Lacey shrugged away from him. It was hard enough to keep her mind on track. Why didn't he button his shirt? "You're taking away all my options. You're even making me seem like a shrew to my children."

"Nothing has changed," Alex insisted. "If anything, you're coming out ahead. You're going to be able to save all the money you've been spending on rent and I'm going to invest some time and money in the farm to help you make it even more profitable."

"Why would you do that?" Had she just stepped into the twilight zone?

"Well, I don't know, Lacey. I hear that guys do that kind of thing for their wives, unless you've decided to back out on me again."

"Me, back out?" She'd passed the twilight zone and was headed to the outer limits. "You called the wedding off last weekend."

"I didn't call off the wedding. I postponed it. I thought you understood. The kids and I need time to get to know each other. That is, if you allow them to be around me. I'm determined to make this work. Eventually, I even intend to break though Jerrod's tough shell."

"Good luck with that."

"So, what about supper tonight?"

Alex turned on his sexy smile, but Lacey wasn't about to give in to him completely, even if it killed her. "How do you feel about meatloaf?"

"I absolutely love meatloaf."

This was good. At least she hadn't erected a brick wall between them. Maybe just a little plaster one. He could break through plaster.

Chapter Fourteen

Lacey was in a silent argument with herself as she mashed the potatoes to smithereens.

Why had she invited Alex for supper?

Well, it would hardly be neighborly to expect the poor man to find his own meal after moving all day. She turned the fire down under a pot of collard greens.

She should have said something about his not calling for five days.

Yeah, right, that wouldn't sound needy and desperate. She slid the meatloaf out of the oven and drained the grease from around it.

If he still intended to marry her, when did he plan to do it? He said he'd only intended to postpone it. He seemed more concerned about how the arrangement affected her kids than she did. She brushed butter over the top of the biscuits and shoved them into the oven.

That wasn't fair. She'd always put the kids first, always.

Well then, why hadn't she come clean about everything? She wasn't innocent in all this.

She'd left the dish towel too close to the stove and a flame burst from its border. Lacey tossed it into the sink and turned on the faucet.

Why should she come clean so soon? He'd hardly seemed interested for the last thirteen years.

Maybe he would have been, if he'd known

everything. She checked the table settings and found two spoons that needed water spots rubbed away.

It had been his choice to leave.

But he said he'd written letters. She lifted the tea pitcher out of the refrigerator and set it on the sideboard.

How many letters can get lost in the mail before you rule out coincidence? Granddad had checked their box at the post office every day.

The greens were turned into a serving bowl for the table. If this was just a game to him, why put so much effort into bonding with the kids. Shouldn't he be trying to win her over first? Don't forget, you're expecting him to accept you all as a package deal. Surely he understands that. And what better way is there to a mother's heart?

A shrill squeal pierced her thoughts, followed by the slamming of the front screen door.

Alex approached the house with a messenger bag over his right shoulder and Jenna tucked under his left arm. He was wearing a white dress shirt with the collar open and the cuffs rolled up. His slacks were sharply creased and his shoes were shined. By the way Jenna's smile beamed up at him, he could have been wearing a suit of armor and riding a trusty white steed. This was one of the many reasons Lacey didn't date. Her daughter craved the male attention she'd never received from a father. She longed to be a Daddy's girl.

Jerrod whipped past her to relieve Alex of his bag. Alex mussed her son's hair and Jerrod swatted his hand away with a good-natured laugh. He actually seemed pleased to see Alex. This was getting worse than she'd anticipated. If Jerrod went over to the enemy camp, who would be on her side?

"Are you spending the weekend, Alex?" Jenna cooed.

"No, honey, I can't," Alex replied. "I still have a lot of unpacking to do. Besides that, I wouldn't want your brother to lose sleep running down the stairs every fifteen minutes to check on me, the way he did last weekend."

Jerrod's face turned red before Alex continued. "I live a lot closer now. It wouldn't be right to impose. I'm just here for a good home cooked meal. In return, I'm planning to take your mom out tomorrow night...with you and Jerrod's permission of course."

Jerrod nodded. "She could use a break. I'll call Granddad and see if we can stay with him. He always makes pan fried steak on Saturday night."

"It takes a damned good man to arrange his own babysitter."

"Hey!" Jerrod objected.

"You're taking Mom on a real date?" Jenna interrupted. "She never goes out. This is so exciting. I know just what she should wear."

"Surprise me." Alex laughed.

"Excuse me," Lacey broke in. "Don't I get a say in this?"

"Obviously not, Sweetheart." Alex gave her a peck on the cheek and walked past her, into the house.

Lacey cursed every annoying little butterfly in her stomach.

****

Alex listened to the chatter at the table and realized that it was all coming from each side of him. Across the table, Lacey picked at her food in quiet contemplation.

What was going on in her pretty little head? Something seemed different about her lately. She seemed a little off focus and looked flushed. Maybe it was just a woman thing. He wasn't used to spending much time with women. It didn't matter though. She was still the sexiest woman he'd ever come across. It would be nice to get her alone for a little while.

"You kids can clean the kitchen tonight," she said, after they'd all finished eating. "Alex and I will take care of the animals while we talk about a few things."

Bingo! She'd read his mind.

"But Mom," Jenna whined, "we've hardly seen Alex for days."

"Don't worry, Sugar," Alex chucked her under the chin, "I won't leave without saying goodnight. Be a good girl and I might bring a surprise for you next time."

Jenna giggled, Lacey growled, and Jerrod rolled his eyes. Alex knew he was a fool for the young girl, but he couldn't help himself. She'd inherited her mother's charm and beauty. Besides that, her adoration for him was a little intoxicating.

Alex took long strides to keep up with Lacey's hurried walk to the barn. Her purposeful steps caused her bottom to bounce perfectly in little red shorts. It took a major amount of willpower not to reach out and cover the back of those shorts with his hands. He knew she was annoyed about something and he'd most likely have to pick himself up off the ground. This would take a little finesse.

The sun had gone down, only leaving a pink glow on the lower half of the horizon. Within the next half hour it would be dark. The barn would be even darker.

He thought about the soft, loose hay covering the floor of the empty stall at the back of the barn. He'd let her say her piece, and then, maybe they could find a use for that stall. Make up sex, reunion sex, Lacey naked, clinging and panting under him. The pictures in his mind were enough to make a man drop to his knees and beg.

She gave each horse a portion of oats from an old plastic pail. She stretched and turned and dipped her body in the graceful movements of a ballerina. With that chore done, she picked up a rake and began smoothing the hay in each stall. "Do you want to grab a bucket and start ladling out water, or are you going to just stand there and watch?"

"I don't know," Alex answered. "The view is pretty good from here."

No snappy reply came back at him, only tight-lipped silence. Alex found a bucket and began filling it from a hose by the door.

"What's the problem, Lacey? You might as well spit it out."

She swung the rake up and slammed the end of the handle onto the ground. A small clump of hay fell from the tines onto her hair. Alex bit back a smile. She shook her head to toss most of the hay off. When the front of her tank top shook as well, his nerves began to vibrate. A small piece of hay lodged in her cleavage to tease him. His mouth went as dry as pocket lint.

"You want to talk to me?" Sarcasm dripped from each word. "After five days without calling, you decide it's time to talk?"

"So, that's the problem?" Alex couldn't believe she was being such a girl. "I was busy moving my whole life and I didn't call, so sue me."

"And that's another thing," Lacey moved closer. "You say you're going to marry me, but you don't even tell me that you're moving. I had to find out from a message on your phone."

"I guess that was wrong. I'm sorry."

"Yes, you are sorry." Angry tears filled her eyes, but she didn't let them fall. "You're here one day and gone the next. It must be a habit of yours. I didn't know if I'd ever see you again. I can't count on you, Alex. The next time you decide to move on, it'll break my kid's hearts. I can't let that happen."

"Exactly what are you saying, Lacey?"

She straightened her shoulders and stuck out her chin. "I'm saying it may not be a good idea to let you get so close. I'd rather you didn't let them hang out at your house."

"For heaven's sake, are you going to think I've left you every time I walk out the door?" Alex pulled his fingers through his hair. "I was just trying to get to know the kids before I end up living with them, which I will at least part-time, after we're married."

"I wouldn't marry you if you were the last man on earth. I'd rather live in my truck. I'll probably end up there anyway, now that you bought the only house in town I could afford to rent."

"Don't you dare cry poor to me, Lacey." The bucket beside Alex's foot overflowed onto his shiny dress shoe. He kicked it over and cursed. As he turned the hose off he continued, "I've seen your books. You bring in a ton of money selling livestock, vegetables, honey, and eggs. You stable horses and give riding lessons. You spend next to nothing after feed and maintenance costs. You've got enough money in the bank to put a twenty percent down payment on this place. Now you tell me, who's being deceitful?"

"That money is going to send my kids to college. I'm not touching a red cent of it! Do you think I want them to work like dogs for the rest of their lives, like me?"

"You call that a college fund?" Alex shouted back. "How many kids do you plan to have?"

"They're all I'll ever have." Lacey's voice was thick with emotion. "That's why I have to do this right."

Alex took a step toward her, but she stepped back and hugged her arms around herself.

"What do you mean by that?" he said in a softer tone. "I don't understand. Make me understand what you just said."

"Why should you care?" she answered in a tiny voice.

"I care a hell of a lot. I care about everything to do with you and I don't like the way you said that. Just tell me what you meant, dammit."

Lacey stiffened her backbone and glared at him. "I'm sorry, Alex, but if we get married, I won't be popping out any little Benson babies. No need to worry about buying an SUV with a big sloppy dog in the window. There wouldn't be any soccer or ballet practices in your future." She turned her back to him. "Maybe you should find someone more suitable."

A lump formed in Alex's throat. He'd never thought he wanted children, but Jenna, and even Jerrod, was starting to get under his skin. Suddenly he felt as though something very precious had been lost. He laid his hands on her shoulders. "What happened?"

Lacey took a deep breath and sighed. "Let's just say the twins' births weren't under ideal circumstances and leave it at that." She turned toward him looking weary and sad. "I'm tired. I need some alone time."

"I understand," Alex pulled her into a hug, as much for his own comfort as hers. He breathed in her sweet scent. She smelled like home. "I'll be back tomorrow, though. I'm not giving up."

"I don't know what you want from me," Lacey whispered.

"I want you to marry me, for no other reason than you want to. I want to get back what we lost all those years ago."

"I need more from you than that, Alex."

"What do you need?" Alex bent his knees to look her in the eye. "Just tell me and it's yours."

"I don't know. I just need…more."

Suddenly a loud clanging sounded from the direction of the house. Alex jumped back. "What the hell is that?"

"It's the emergency bell." Lacey jogged toward the door. "Someone's in trouble."

Chapter Fifteen

Alex's heart thundered as he raced through the back door behind Lacey. The only light in the house was in the living room. As they reached the doorway, they could see Jenna and Jerrod sitting quietly on the sofa, side by side. They looked thunderstruck, but why? There didn't seem to be a fire, no flood, no blood.

"What's going on in here?" Alex's voice boomed louder than he'd intended.

"So, what the boy told me is true."

Lacey visibly jumped at the sound of her grandfather's voice coming from a chair turned away from them.

Clarence Carlyle stood and slowly faced them. "You two are at it again. At least you had enough sense to take him to the barn with the other animals. Your children don't need to witness your shameless behavior," he sneered.

"That's enough, Mr. Carlyle," Alex snapped.

"Didn't you get the message all those years ago, young man? You're not needed around here. You'll bring nothing but heartache to my family, just like you did before."

"What are you talking about, Granddad?" Lacey asked. "What message?"

Alex never looked away from the old man. He knew without having to ask.

"I'm cleaning the trash out of my house." Clarence reached for a large old shoebox on the side table. "I brought you your part of it, boy. Now take it and go. Don't ever come back here."

He removed the lid and emptied the box on the floor. A pile of envelopes grew around Alex's feet. They were all unopened and yellowed with age. Alex recognized them, though. They had the U.S. Navy logo on the top corner and Carlyle's address was written in his own handwriting.

Lacey dropped to her knees and gathered handfuls of the letters. She looked as though she were in a trance. She was barely breathing. Suddenly, she let out a frustrated scream. Jenna whimpered and called for her in a tiny voice, but Lacey's eyes had narrowed onto her grandfather. An expression of sheer hatred soured her pretty face.

"Why did you do this?" she shrieked. "I needed these and you took them. You're an evil, horrible man."

"Don't you talk to me that way," Clarence bellowed. "My son's life was ruined because of you, and still I took you in."

"How can you say that?" Lacey sobbed as she clutched an armful of the letters to her chest.

"He was my only son, my only child. He was all I had. He would have followed in my footsteps. But then your mother came along and turned his head. She got pregnant for you and I lost him. He could have been somebody, but instead he chose to make a living digging in the dirt, just like you're doing. When he was gone, I got saddled with you, a moody, ungrateful little snot. It didn't take you long to turn into a trollop, just like your mother."

Alex's hands opened and closed repeatedly at his sides. He wanted to make a fist to drive through Clarence's face. But the old man was too fragile and the kids didn't need to witness such violence.

Jerrod jumped to his feet. Tears ran unashamedly down his cheeks. "I won't have you talking to my mom that way, Granddad. You'd better leave. You're the one who's not welcome here."

"You won't talk to me that way, boy," Clarence growled. "I'll take my belt off to you."

"You touch either one of these kids and I'll rip your heart out and feed it to you." Alex's voice came out like a clap of thunder. "You've done all the damage you're going to, old man. Now, get the hell off of my property."

Minutes later, Alex stood on the front porch, feet spread and arms folded. He watched Mr. Carlyle's car turn onto the road and disappear. Beside him, Jerrod stood in a matching pose. Even Buck looked satisfied as he sat at the foot of the steps looking out.

"Rip his heart out and feed it to him? I like it. Thanks, Alex."

Alex grabbed the boy in a headlock and ruffled his curly hair. "Don't mention it, kid. It took a lot of balls to stand up for your mom, the way you did. I'm proud of you."

The male bonding moment was cut short when Jenna stepped out the front door. "Alex, I'm not sure if mom is okay. She's crying a lot."

Alex dropped his head with a sigh. "I'll take her upstairs and help her get ready for bed. Can you make her a cup of tea and bring it up?"

"Sure."

Before Jerrod could follow Jenna into the house, Alex took his arm and held him back. "Look, I know I said I wasn't staying, but I can't leave her like this," he whispered. "I'm going to spend the night, and I'm going to sleep in her room. Is that going to cause a problem with you?"

"I guess, if it's okay with her, it'll be okay with me. But you are going to leave the door open, right?"

Alex chuckled and shoved Jerrod through the door ahead of him. "If we didn't already have Buck, you'd make a great guard dog, boy."

In her room, Alex settled Lacey into her bed, and then stripped down to his T-shirt and boxers. He slid under the covers beside her and sat with his back against the headboard. He pulled her against his chest to rest her head on his shoulder.

Lacey was half asleep, but her breath still caught in occasional gasps from crying so hard.

Now that the truth had come out about his letters, things would be different. They could finally get back on track.

A tap sounded on the door and he looked up to see Jenna with Lacey's tea.

"Come on in, sugar."

Jenna handed Alex the cup and watched as he held it to her mother's lips. "Mom will probably kick my butt for saying so," she whispered, "but you look good there. She needs somebody like you to help her out sometimes."

Alex smiled. "Good night, Jenna," he said in a low, teasing voice.

"Good night, Alex," she mimicked. She walked back through the door and began to pull it closed.

"Jenna. You can leave the door open."

Jerrod had been man enough to stand up for his mom.

There was no need to drive him crazy.

Chapter Sixteen

Alex was technically awake, but he refused to open his eyes. Once he did, the spell would be broken. He'd have to get out of bed and start his day. Nothing in the world felt better than he did at that moment. He hated to give up the warm softness of Lacey's body against his.

Lacey had been his only real relationship before the accident, and they'd had to sneak even a kiss. In all his thirty-two years he'd never slept an entire night with a woman in his arms. She fit him perfectly, from her head tucked under his chin to her round bottom snuggled between his legs. It was no wonder that he'd slept more soundly then he had in years.

Her scent was a mixture of wild flowers, sunshine, and clean linen. He buried his nose in her hair to inhale it deeper. Perhaps it would lull him back to sleep.

"Mom?" a soft whisper came from over his shoulder. "Mom…"

Alex grudgingly opened one eye and rolled toward the intruder. He slid his legs over the edge of the mattress and sat up pulling a pillow over his lap. Now was not the time to discuss morning wood with a preadolescent boy.

He scrubbed his hands over his face, and then let them travel through his hair. He looked at Jerrod through that one squinted eye. "What time is it?" he whispered.

"It's almost seven o'clock," Jerrod whispered back. "I've already done my chores and Jenna is just about finished with hers. Mom's usually up by now. Is she okay?"

"She had a rough night. I think she could use a little more sleep." Now that Alex had things under control he tucked his pillow against her back. "What's the problem?"

"Well," Jerrod shrugged sheepishly, "I'm hungry and Jenna is threatening to make breakfast. I'm not exaggerating when I say that you could sink a battleship with one of her biscuits. She always gets shells in the eggs and burns the bacon. I can make coffee, but that's about it for my cooking skills."

"Put the coffee on, kid. I'll clean up and be down in a minute." Now that Alex had his body under control, he stood and stretched. "You and Jenna are about to get a crash course in how to make breakfast the Benson way."

When Jerrod had left the room, Alex turned back to look at Lacey. She looked like a life-sized doll as she slept on her side, all curled up. Her hands were pressed together under her cheek and her feet were peeking out from under the sheet. He noticed the way her lips were slightly opened in a sexy pucker. He'd pay a million bucks to have those soft perfect lips touch every inch of his body.

Dammit, he had to get a lock for that door.

****

When Lacey opened her eyes the sun was above the tree line outside her window. She figured the time must be after nine. She hadn't slept this late since the twins had been born.

She'd awakened once during the night and found Alex's arms around her. She'd stayed as still as a statue not to wake him. She couldn't face him after what had transpired in her living room last night. The things her grandfather said, the letters he'd kept from her. She had accused Alex of lying and it had been her own grandfather who had deceived her. The sad thing was, she wasn't surprised. He'd said horrible things about Alex all along.

Last night, Alex hadn't only witnessed her grandfather's ghastly behavior; he'd seen her fall apart. Strong, responsible Lacey had come apart at the seams. He'd had to take care of her, carry her to bed, and feed her tea. How could she ever face him again? He'd probably raced for the door before daybreak.

Looking in the bathroom mirror, she saw that her eyes were still a little swollen. She pressed a cold, wet cloth to them. She'd just started brushing her teeth when sounds came from downstairs loud enough to be a herd of buffalo in her kitchen. They were accompanied by a chorus of howls and laughter. What were those kids doing?

With toothbrush in hand, she raced down the stairs and into the kitchen. Sliding to a stop in the doorway, Lacey found Jerrod lying on his back in the middle of the floor. Alex was over the top of him with Jenna on his back. It was an Alex sandwich. They were all laughing hysterically.

Lacey nearly choked on her toothpaste when she saw Jerrod's face covered in peanut butter. All three offenders froze in place and turned looks of wide-eyed innocence her way. They slowly got to their feet and faced her.

"We really screwed up this time, kids," Alex mumbled. "She's so mad, she frothing at the mouth."

Both kids turned red and covered their mouths. Their eyes watered from the effort it took not to laugh.

Lacey rinsed her mouth, and then picked up the overturned peanut butter jar. "Would someone please tell me, what's going on?"

Alex cleared his throat and squared his shoulders. He gave her a serious expression. "I'm sorry. I had no choice. Your son called me a sissy. He had to be punished."

Jerrod scraped a finger down his cheek and into his mouth, looking unrepentant. "I stand by what I said, Mom. The man wears hair gel."

"I tried to stop them," Jenna added. "I was just getting ready to make lunch."

"Lunch! What time is it?" She checked the clock above the stove. It was eleven-thirty.

Alex was still glaring at Jerrod. "If I didn't gel my hair it would look like that mop on your head," he growled.

"I want you kids cleaned up in fifteen minutes," Lacey demanded. "I'm sure Alex has his own work to get back to."

The twins left the room grumbling under their breaths.

"It sounds like you're kicking me out," Alex said. "If it's because of the peanut butter thing…"

"It has nothing to do with peanut butter. I've just got a lot to do and I need some time to think without you crowding me."

Alex looked like he'd just been slapped. "I do have some things to get done, but next time you get mad at me, we're going to talk it out. You can't keep pushing me away, then get upset because you haven't heard from me. It's not fair and I'm not going to put up with it much longer."

"What's that supposed to mean? Are you threatening to leave again?"

"What that means is…you can't always have everything your way. When we're married, I won't be your lap dog."

"No need to worry. I'm not ever going to marry you."

"Why?"

"I've already told you. This just isn't enough."

"Oh, right," he replied with sarcasm. "You want more, the magical, mysterious more. Has it ever occurred to you that we all want more? I know I do." Alex backed her against the wall with his forward movement, stopping only inches from touching her. "Every time I look in your eyes, I feel like I'm soaring through a clear blue sky."

He bunched the back of her hair in his hand. "Every time I see your hair I want to touch it, smell it, and rub it against my face. I dream about what it would look like spread across my pillow. When you speak, my eyes are drawn to your lips." He lightly kissed her. "I want to taste the honey sweetness of your mouth. I want to steal your breath for my own. I want to hear you whisper my name like a lover."

Alex drew the strap of Lacey's nightgown off her shoulder, exposing the top of her soft round breast where he placed another small kiss. "Your scent drives me insane with the need to taste every inch of you until you beg for more."

His hand traveled up her leg, just to the edge of her panties. "When I touch you, I want to bury myself so deeply inside you that we no longer qualify as two separate people. I want to drive myself in your silky tightness until you come apart in my arms and drain me."

Lacey's eyes felt sleepy. Her chest rose and fell with every rapid breath. Her light cotton gown felt constricting. She ached to touch Alex, to kiss him, to give him all he'd asked for.

A thump from overhead drew both their attention. It reminded them they weren't alone. The kids could be back in an instant.

"We don't always get what we want." Alex grabbed his keys from his pocket. "When you figure out what *more* is to you, give me a call."

Lacey watched from the living room window as Alex drove away. She knew she'd overreacted and come off like a shrew. Why couldn't she control herself around him? How had her life gotten so complicated?

She ran upstairs and quickly changed into a blouse and jeans. She had work to do, unlike some people.

When she returned to the kitchen, Jenna was quietly making sandwiches at the counter. She didn't face her mother. Lacey knew the kids were going through almost as much turmoil as she was. She'd have to find a way to smooth things over for them, but right now she had more pressing matters to pursue. She pulled the truck keys off the peg by the door.

"Hold down the fort for me, honey. I'll be at Granddad's house if you need me."

"Mom." Jenna swung around in near panic. "Are you sure you should go by yourself?"

"Jenna, last night is history. I can't say I'm over it, but I can handle it. I've dealt with Clarence Carlyle for years. He can't hurt me anymore than he already has. Now, it's about damned time he gave me some answers."

Chapter Seventeen

Lacey didn't bother to knock on her grandfather's door. This had been her home at one time, and he was her family. She walked straight through the house until she found him in the kitchen.

His back was to her as he poured himself a cup of coffee. He poured a second cup and brought them both to the table. If Lacey didn't know better, she'd think he'd been expecting her. How would he know she'd ever speak to him again?

Clarence sat at the table and silently poured cream in his cup from the little pitcher in the center of the table. He blew into his coffee, and then took a sip. "Have a seat. You make me nervous, just standing there."

Lacey had always obeyed her grandfather. It was a habit she'd been taught from childhood. A person respected their elders no matter how bad they were. She sat across from him and said the first thing that popped into her mind. "What is wrong with you, Granddad?" Respect only stretched so far.

Clarence didn't have to ask what she meant, he knew. "Funny, you should ask, I've been wondering the same thing for years."

Was that self-loathing she heard in his voice? Oh no, she would not let him turn this around on her. She would not feel sorry for him. She was the one who'd been hurt by *his* actions.

"I always knew you didn't like me. But I had no idea how much you hated me. You even hated my mother, and all she ever did was love my dad. You barely tolerate Jerrod and you don't have anything to do with Jenna." A lump formed in Lacey's throat and tears burned her eyes. "My dad may have been the only person you ever cared about, but even that wore thin before he died. You were so tough on him. Have you always hated everyone? What made you so angry and unyielding?"

As much as Lacey willed her grandfather to look her in the eye, he wouldn't. He stared into his coffee cup. She began to wonder if he'd ever answer. Finally he did.

"I loved your father. That's why I was hard on him. I didn't want him to end up like me."

"You wanted him to be exactly like you. You wanted him to be a businessman and care about nothing else. You wanted him to be cold and closed off. You hated that he fell in love."

"Yes, I did. Nothing good comes from it. It's not real. All you get is pain."

"How can you say that?" Lacey was truly shocked by his claim. "You must have loved my grandmother, the result being my father. It's a shame you had to lose her so early, but it happens and you have to move on."

Clarence huffed. It couldn't have been a chuckle because he didn't look amused. He looked sad. Then, he said something that truly shocked Lacey. "Did someone tell you that your grandmother died, or is that just an assumption?"

Lacey thought back to the only time she'd asked

about her grandmother. It had been during a conversation with her mother. "Your dad lost his mom at a very young age. He doesn't even remember her." Lost, exactly what did that mean?

"I guess I just assumed," Lacey mumbled. She wasn't sure she wanted to hear the truth.

"When I met Maggie I was twenty-two. I was a handsome man then, and I had plenty of girls chasing after me. I'd never felt an instant attraction to any woman the way I did her, though. It was on a Saturday. Our church was hosting a picnic for the church in Citrus. Maggie came off that church bus wearing a dress with pink flowers all over it. She had on one of those pillbox hats. Her hair was the same color as yours. I'd just gotten a job as a teller at the bank. I guess that's why I mustered up the courage to talk to her. I was feeling like a big man. The way she smiled at me…"

During his pause, Lacey didn't know what to say. She'd never seen such a dreamy expression on her grandfather's wrinkled old face.

"Anyway," he went on, "I went about courting her. She was almost twenty and lived at home. Although they seemed to be nice enough people, she was unhappy living with her parents. She said they were too strict and she wanted to get out in the world. It only took me a few months to ask her to marry me. I was so taken with her I couldn't wait. By the very next year, John, your father, came along. I was so proud I could have popped my vest buttons. However, Maggie was already getting restless. She constantly complained that we didn't have enough money. I'd work harder at the bank to try to get a raise, and she complained that I was never home. I desperately wanted to make her happy.

"My hard work at the bank paid off. John was two-years old the day I was made Loan Manager. I came home early. I wanted to take her out for dinner at the diner in town to celebrate. One of the neighbor ladies was here, taking care of John. Maggie was out shopping. I found out she went shopping every Friday afternoon. I waited for hours. When she came home she was wearing that same pink flowered dress she'd worn the day I met her. She also had on a new gold necklace shaped like a heart. She told me she bought it for herself with some of the money she'd saved using coupons. I believed her."

When he paused again, Lacey didn't think she wanted to hear any more. Then, she decided this might be exactly what her grandfather needed. She poured them each more coffee.

"She was happy with the extra money for a little while," Clarence continued. "But you know how it is. With some people, it's never enough. Soon, we were fighting more than ever. It was a Wednesday when I came home to find the same neighbor as before watching John. He was three-years-old by then. She told me she'd been watching him almost every day for months. I waited for hours again. Finally I decided to change clothes. That's when I saw that her side of the closet was empty." He lifted his hands, palms up, and shrugged.

Lacey couldn't leave it at that. She had to know the rest of what had poisoned her grandfather's life. "Did you ever hear from her after that?" Her voice felt as weak as her grandfather looked.

"Two years later." Clarence took a deep breath.

"She called from a honky-tonk in Texas. She was drunk. She wanted a thousand dollars. She said I owed it to her for stealing her youth." He chuckled. "I wonder how much she thought my heart was worth, because she'd taken it with her when she left. I didn't divorce her until after that call."

"You never loved anyone after she'd gone?"

"No. I'd never let myself be such a fool a second time. I'd been weak and vulnerable. I didn't want that for your father, but I couldn't tell him about his mother and he wouldn't listen to reason anyway. When I learned what was happening between you and the Benson boy, I wanted to spare you that pain too."

"But you didn't, Granddad. Instead of Alex, it was you that broke my heart. I don't know if I can ever get past that." Lacey walked to the sink with her cup. She rinsed it out and set it on the counter. Without turning to face him, she added, "I don't know why, but I love you. I'm sure the kids do too. You're all the family we have. We're all you have. I'm sorry for what happened, but I want you to think about how you want the future to play out. Think about how different it could be, if you were to put the past behind you."

"Leopards don't change their spots, Lacey."

"Your spots were painted on by your own brush. My grandmother had no right to treat you that way, but you had no right to make everyone around you suffer for it. Now, you can wash those spots off and start living again, or you can die a lonely old man. It's your choice."

On her way home, Lacey chided herself for not taking her own advice. Maybe it was time for her to forgive the past as well.

She wanted to move forward. Perhaps that's why she still hadn't opened any of Alex's letters. But could she say, after all these years that Alex was definitely the man for her? All her feelings for him were tied to their past, or she thought they were.

She needed time to think, time to figure out what was holding her back, what was missing.

Chapter Eighteen

Alex paced the floor in his private sitting room. He couldn't concentrate on a book. When he tried to watch a television program his mind wandered and he lost track of the story line. Thank goodness he'd had his work and unpacking to keep him busy earlier. Otherwise he would have gone bonkers by now.

He'd tried to call Lacey on Saturday to set up their date for that night, but Jenna answered. After leaving him waiting for several minutes, she'd said her mom wasn't feeling well and planned to go to bed early. She didn't feel up to going out.

On the third attempt Sunday, he got through to Jerrod. The boy explained that he and his sister had been at church that morning, and then gone fishing in the afternoon. He said his mom had just gone upstairs to take a bath and he would tell her to call back. She didn't call.

Now it was Monday evening. Alex was determined to wait for Lacey to make the next move. He wasn't going to act like a love struck teenager.

Maybe Lacey was right to take time to think things over. Perhaps he should do the same. His original intentions had flown out the window the minute he'd touched his lips to hers. His body came to attention, just from the memory. Things were moving too quickly.

Alex decided he'd gone too far when he'd accused

her of making him her lap dog. Or perhaps it was that inexplicable *more* that was coming between them. He definitely should have kept his hands to himself, but he'd had a head of steam and once he started he couldn't stop himself. Dammit, why couldn't women make sense?

Wearing only a white ribbed undershirt and boxers, Alex passed his reflection in the mirror. He rubbed his right palm over his left shoulder and down his arm. Maybe the *more* she needed was a man that hadn't had so much of himself burned away.

How long had it taken for him to be able to touch his own scars without feeling nauseated?

Sure, she could be clinical and compassionate about it in the light of day, but maybe this isn't what she wants to hold on to in the night. Could he blame her?

Alex pulled on a pair of old blue sweatpants. He exchanged the undershirt for a long-sleeved gray T-shirt. It wouldn't be the first time he'd gone for a run at night to burn off negative energy. At least Indian Lakes was safer than Orlando and had a lot less traffic.

To his surprise, the front doorbell rang. Maybe an old friend had heard he was back in town. He hadn't had time to socialize since he moved in. He didn't care if it was a vacuum cleaner salesman or a Bible thumper. Anything would be better than driving himself crazy worrying about Lacey.

He found Jenna standing on his doorstep wearing a backpack. She had a pillow under one arm and a beat-up teddy bear under the other.

"What are you doing out at this time of night?" She walked past him and laid her things in the nearest chair.

"Were you planning to move in?"

"I was at Stacy's house for a sleepover, but then I started feeling really sick." Her bottom lip poked out. "Maybe I ate too much raw cookie dough."

"That would do it for me," Alex grumbled. "Does your mom know you're here?"

"No, I was just down the street and I thought I'd see if you could take me home." She looked at him with innocent, puppy dog eyes. "If I call Mom, I'll have to wait for her to get here before I can get back to the farm."

"If I drive you, are you going to barf in my beemer?" Alex cringed.

"I promise I won't," Jenna smiled. "But if it'll make you feel better, I'll carry a plastic bag."

"I'll get my wallet and keys," Alex sighed, "You get the plastic bag."

****

Lacey had been avoiding Alex for days, but she could hardly refuse to open the door to him when he had her daughter in tow. Her motherly concern overruled her embarrassment, and really that's all it was. She'd been embarrassed by her weakness when she'd seen his letters. She'd been embarrassed that she allowed him to lie in her bed and hold her the whole night. Her life was out of control and Alex had a front row seat to witness it.

After Jenna was tucked into her bed and checked over, Alex kissed the girl on the forehead. "At least she's not running a fever. I hope she feels better soon."

"Oh, I'm sure she'll feel better by tomorrow," Lacey replied drolly. She knew when her kids were sick and when they were faking. Jenna was definitely faking. But why?

She turned off the light and went back down the stairs. Alex followed. As soon as her foot left the bottom step he said, "You broke our date."

"I don't remember you asking me on a date."

"I wasn't going to force you to go out with me. You had your chance to say no. So what's the problem? Did you decide you didn't want to be seen with me in public?"

Lacey suddenly remembered his scars. He'd told her how people had reacted to them in the past, especially women. She couldn't let him think she was like them. All she could think to do was tell him the truth. "It's not that I didn't want to go." She groped for the right words. "The truth is…I was embarrassed."

"Embarrassed, by what?" He narrowed his eyes and tightened his jaw as if preparing himself for a blow.

She was handling this badly. "I don't usually break down like that. You must think I'm an emotional train wreck."

"Do you remember our first kiss?" His body visibly relaxed and his eyes softened. "It was after your parents' funeral." He stepped closer and she stepped back. "You were devastated." He came closer still and she kept backing away. Why did she keep resisting him? "Mrs. Dell made that nasty comment and you ran to the woods by the lake. That's where we found our secret place."

The back of her legs came in contact with the edge of the sofa. Alex gently lowered her down and knelt in front of her. "I followed you. I thought you were the most beautiful girl I'd ever seen, tears and all." Alex moved up to kiss her. A soft touch on her arm, a little nudge on her shoulder, and she found herself lying on her back. "I kissed you and we made love for the first time."

Lacey did remember. It had been the most incredible night of her life, and yet, Alex the boy couldn't compare to the man that kissed her now. His kiss was soft and tender, slow and gentle. Her ears buzzed and she felt as though warm honey ran through her veins.

When his lips left hers, she whimpered from the feeling of abandonment, but the warmth of his body stayed with her. His hands started at her quivering belly and slowly moved up. Her shirt and bra moved with them. The hot wet touch of his mouth on her breasts caused a sensation in her body she'd almost forgotten existed. The tug of his lips caused her back to bow, begging for more. Instead of words, she released another pleading whimper. He answered with a growl.

He trailed kisses down her stomach, stopping to lick her belly button. She knew it was a promise of better things to come. When his hands gripped each sides of her waistband her hips instinctively rose.

Suddenly, the back screen door slammed in the kitchen. She'd forgotten that Jerrod would be coming in from the barn. This couldn't be happening again.

"You have to go." Tugging her clothes into place was difficult with his body hovering over hers. She pushed him away and stood.

Alex took a deep breath and looked down at her. The tight bulge in his pants revealed his intention and frustration.

"I'm being as patient with you as I know how, Lacey," he whispered. "But sooner or later, I'm liable to go very caveman on you. There's only so much I can take."

Lacey had just closed the door behind him when Jerrod called out. "Do we have anything to eat?"

"Help yourself to some leftover cornbread and honey. Jenna came home sick and I need to see to her."

After taking several minutes to calm her nerves, Lacey leaned against the doorframe to Jenna's bedroom. "Perhaps I should give you a nice big dose of castor oil before you go to sleep."

"Mom, no, really. That would only make me feel worse."

"You're no sicker than I am. What is up in that devious little mind of yours?"

Jenna sat up and pretended to pick lint from her comforter to keep from making eye contact. "I just wanted you and Alex to get back together. I thought if I could get him over here, the two of you might...talk...and maybe kiss...and hug...and stuff like that."

"You shouldn't be thinking about stuff like that." Lacey went to her daughter's bedside and turned on her little lamp.

"Honey, please don't do this." Lacey sat on the edge of the bed and smoothed her hand down Jenna's braid. "Alex isn't part of my life anymore. Maybe, he never will be."

"But he's part of mine, isn't he, Mom? How long am I supposed to pretend I don't know?"

Lacey sprang from the bed and closed the door. She turned back to Jenna. Trying to keep her voice even, she asked, "What is it that you think you know, sweetheart?"

"Mom, please don't treat me like an infant," Jenna pouted. "I see the way you and Alex look at each other. The letters Granddad brought yesterday proved I was right. Alex is my dad."

"You read the letters?"

"Of course not! But I did read the envelopes. There were dozens of them. They were dated from July to November of the year we were born. I did the math."

Jenna had always been a smart girl. Lacey knew she could no longer deny the truth. "Does your brother know?"

"Not yet. I wanted you to tell us both."

"I'm sorry, Jenna." Shame washed over Lacey like cold water. "I've made some big mistakes. Please don't say anything to Jerrod yet. You know how he tends to fly off the handle. I have to think about how I can break this to him gently."

"What about Alex? He doesn't know yet, does he?"

"No, and that's going to be even harder. Just give me a little time." Lacey leaned over and kissed Jenna's cheek then turned to leave.

"Mom," Jenna said as she wiggled back under the covers, "were Jerrod and I one of your big mistakes?"

Lacey gasped and had to hold back tears. "No, baby. You two were a wonderful surprise."

"I hope Alex thinks so too," Jenna said in a sleepy voice.

Chapter Nineteen

Lacey tightened the lids on the jars of preserves. She'd barely slept for two nights in a row. She'd lain awake at night trying to decide what to do about her dilemma.

Alex would be furious, and she wouldn't blame him. He might even leave again, and that would break her heart as much as the first time. The other thing that worried her was that Jerrod would feel betrayed. She'd have to face his distrust and disdain every day for as long as he lived at home. What kind of relationship would they have, once he was grown? Would it be like the one she shared with her grandfather? She stood to lose both of the most important men in her life.

After the hours of internal deliberation, Lacey decided to meet with Alex privately. Once he was over the shock-if he got over it-she'd ask him to help her talk to Jerrod. Maybe it was the coward's way out, but she couldn't handle it alone, not this time.

After telling Jerrod she'd be in town for a little while, Lacey started up her old truck and drove straight to Osceola Lane. A wide space at the side of Alex's house had been covered with gravel and surrounded by a low rail fence for parking. Alex's BMW was the only car there. He must have closed the office for lunch, thank heavens. She didn't need an audience for this conversation.

At the bottom of the porch steps, a new sign had been made for his business. It was an old-fashioned standing sign that better suited the style of the old Victorian house. He was making an effort to fit in with the community.

The front door swung open before she could reach it. Alex stood wearing business casual slacks, an open collared dress shirt, and a smile. "I'm glad to see you're not avoiding me. I guess you just couldn't resist me anymore, right?"

Lacey followed him into the house. It was obvious that business had started in the new office. The desks were cluttered with pens, paper clips, mail, messages and file folders. Large rolled up plans were stacked in a rolling cart by the filing cabinets. Magazines littered the side tables in the sitting area. The trash baskets were half full. She was lucky to catch him alone this time, but she'd remember to call ahead before coming by again.

"I don't know how you could move an entire company in less than two weeks. How do you plan to get business in such a small town?" Lacey asked.

"This isn't my whole company," Alex chuckled. "It's more like a command center for my satellite offices. They do the real work. I just oversee the paperwork and bookkeeping and such. I can do that from anywhere, and I've decided to do it from here. I still have to travel to the other offices occasionally, but this is home base."

"How many satellite offices do you have?" Lacey was awestruck.

"Let's see." He counted on his fingers. "There are three in Florida, three in Georgia, one in South

Carolina, one in North Carolina, and two in Virginia, ten all together."

"How many people do you employ?" Her voice was embarrassingly breathy.

"I don't really know. Each office has its own payroll account for office staff, agents, construction workers, developers, and so on. There's probably a report, somewhere around here, for that."

"Shit, Alex," Lacey squeaked, "you must be like a millionaire."

Alex's eyes twinkled when he grinned. "Cool, huh? Would you like to go upstairs and see my etchings?" He pulled her close and nibbled at the side of her neck.

"You don't draw." Lacey giggled.

"Oh, is that what etchings are?" He nipped her ear. "I could start, with the right redheaded model."

She squirmed in his arms. "You can't afford me," she said in a hoity-toity tone.

"I'm a wealthy man." He gently cupped her breast. "But you would have to pose nude."

Lacey's next giggle caught in her throat when she heard the back door open and a woman's voice rang out, "Alex, where are you? I saw a truck in the drive. Are you with a client?"

They jumped apart as Donna Sullivan stepped through the kitchen door with two grocery bags. It was midday, but her makeup was heavily applied and her bleached hair was teased to an unbelievable height. She teetered on stiletto heels, showing miles of bare legs below her tight miniskirt.

"Well, Lacey Carlyle." Her heavy southern accent put Lacey in mind of Blanche from "A Streetcar Named Desire". "I run across your kids every now and then, but I hardly ever see you. Are you thinking of buying a new place? I had to pick up some cream. I just cannot make myself drink coffee black the way Alex does. I also got some diet soda. Can I offer you one?"

Donna certainly seemed at home in Alex's house.

"No thanks, I was just leaving. I have tons of things to do. I'll leave you two alone. See you later." Much later, she promised herself.

Alex followed her to the door. "You never said why you came by."

"Just visiting." She didn't bother to face him as she walked out the door. "I've really got to get going, but I'll talk to you later."

****

Alex ran back to Donna, grabbed her up and swung her around. "She's jealous! She's absolutely, positively, unequivocally jealous! She wants me whether she admits it or not." He smacked a big kiss on her heavily rouged cheek.

"Well, go after her, you idiot, I mean…boss." She smacked him away playfully.

"No way. She's been giving me hell lately. I'm going to let her stew for a while."

****

Lacey stopped at the dollar store for a few cleaning products. She ran by the local grocery for some basic staples, and then checked out a couple of books from the library. Still, her blood pressure was high. She tried to cool her anger by driving around, but continued to grumble, cuss and bang her fist against the steering wheel.

How could Alex kiss her the way he had, and say the things he did, then spend his time, doing who knows what, with Donna Sullivan, her complete opposite? Did he really expect the three of them to sit down and have coffee together? Their relationship would be from an arm's distance, or more, from now on. She wasn't anyone's fool.

By the time she turned into the Double J, it was a quarter to three. Jenna was standing on the front porch, looking out across the pasture. She parked the truck. Jenna ran toward her with an expression of relief. She'd left the kids alone for over four hours. The longest she'd ever allowed. They were probably worried the truck had broken down.

"Where have you been, Mom?" Jenna exclaimed. "I wanted to call, but I didn't know where you were."

"I told Jerrod I had to run some errands. Didn't he tell you?" Lacey was surprised by Jenna's obvious distress.

"Jerrod rode out just after you left."

"What do you mean he rode out? He knows better than to leave the house when I'm gone."

"He said he was going to check on the new calves in the east pasture, and he wanted to give Drifter a workout, but he didn't come back for lunch." Jenna was nearly in tears. "It's not like him to miss a meal. I've got a bad feeling about this."

Lacey paused a moment before she spoke. "Was Jerrod upset about anything?"

"No. He seemed perfectly normal. I promise I haven't said anything to him, just like you asked."

Lacey hated asking Jenna to keep such a secret. It was a heavy burden on the girl to not share something so important with her twin. Now she'd have to rethink her strategy with Jerrod. He had every right to know the truth.

At this moment, though, she just wanted to find her son. And she intended to kick his scrawny butt the minute she did. "You know what? I bet Jerrod took a lunch with him. He probably snuck out to go skinny-dipping and fell asleep under a tree."

As the minutes, and then hours ticked slowly by, Lacey itched to saddle Stardust and ride out to find Jerrod, but Jenna was silent and edgy. She couldn't leave the girl alone. She wished her granddad hadn't gone to his lodge meeting.

The table was set for supper and the food was getting cold on the back of the stove. Neither she nor Jenna had an appetite. Lacey finally jerked the phone from its cradle and called the sheriff.

"Lacey, darlin', you know that boy is just goofing off somewhere," the sheriff's dispatcher, Gladys, said after hearing Lacey's account of what was happening.

"He's been gone over seven hours, Gladys. How long will it be before someone cares?"

"Honey, with Jerrod being as old as he is, we have to wait twenty-four hours to take an official report. A lot of kids run off, but then they change their mind once it gets dark or they start getting hungry."

"He didn't run off!" Lacey was getting angrier by the minute.

"Our cars are all tied up right now at an accident out by the highway, but I tell you what," Gladys sighed, "I'll send someone out to check on y'all in a few hours."

Lacey felt dizzy, her ears were buzzing, but she had to hold herself together for her kids. "Thanks, Gladys. I'll be sure to let everyone know how helpful

the department has been…right about election time."
She slammed the phone back into its cradle.

Chapter Twenty

Alex practically flew his BMW out to the Double J. Lacey had tried to sound calm and casual when she'd called, but he could hear the fear underlying her words. The bottom line: Jerrod was missing. He'd left at about eleven that morning and hadn't been seen since.

Jerrod could be a boneheaded little monster, but he wasn't irresponsible. Actually, he was the most responsible kid Alex had ever known. He wouldn't run away. Taking care of his mother and the farm were his top priorities, not to mention his closeness to his twin sister. Hell, they had their own sign language.

Why weren't the cops looking for him? As soon as this mess was cleared up, he intended to have an answer to that question. There were perks to being wealthy and he'd damned sure take advantage of them.

Before the car came to a stop, Lacey and Jenna jumped from the front porch without touching a step. On closer inspection, he saw they'd both been crying.

"I've called all the neighbors and Jerrod's friends. No one has seen him. They're all searching their properties, the woods in between, and the roads." Lacey still had the cordless house phone gripped in her hand.

"The sun will be down in another hour," Jenna cried. "Jerrod's never been outdoors alone all night."

Alex pried Lacey's fingers from the phone and handed it to Jenna. "Is there a good horse we could saddle quickly?"

"I've already saddled Stardust. I was just waiting for you. I can't leave Jenna alone. I can't sit here and wait any longer."

Alex gripped Lacey by the shoulders. "Look me in the eye. Tell me who the best tracker in the county used to be when we all went out hunting."

"You were," she answered meekly.

"I could find anything, man as well as beast. I still can. But right now, time is wasting." He looked past her to include Jenna. "I need a good flashlight, a first aid kit, and bottled water. Most important, I need that horse."

The women gathered all he'd asked for, plus a bag of leftover chicken and biscuits. Alex checked over the mare and within minutes he was mounted. He pulled back on Stardust's reins to move her away from the railing. "You two stay by the phone in case anyone finds anything. I'll call you when I've got Jerrod. I will find him, I promise. I'm not coming back until I do."

****

As Alex rode away, Lacey finally felt like something was being done. Alex hadn't talked down to her as though she were a hysterical child. He'd evaluated the situation seriously and taken charge. She hadn't even had to ask. All she'd told him was that Jerrod was missing and he'd sprung into action. He hadn't laid blame, tried to cajole her, or asked for anything in return. This is what it would be like to have a man in her life, a helpmate.

She prayed that daylight would hold out long enough. She prayed Alex would find her boy safe and healthy. Jerrod was her baby. He always would be. If

Alex could bring her son home, she'd give him anything. The wait was excruciating.

"I should be out there too," Lacey moaned.

"Mom, please trust Alex. I do. He's a good man and he'll do everything possible to bring Jerrod back safely." Jenna looked out in the direction she'd given Alex. "He may not know about us yet, but he's already the best dad I know."

****

The ground was so hard and dry; there was hardly any trail to follow. It hadn't rained in days. All Alex could track were broken sticks, beaten down weeds, and the freshest horse droppings. Not even that was reliable once he entered the outer pasture that the cattle had grazed all day.

To the west, Alex caught that single second when the sun appears to melt into the horizon. Now the sky was a shade of lavender that would quickly turn violet, purple, and then the darkest indigo. If he were looking for a grown man, he'd consider delaying the search until morning.

Jerrod was strong, fearless, and probably capable of running this farm single-handedly. He was also a child. Alex hadn't ever asked his age, but he knew the kids hadn't entered their teens. According to Jenna, they were still in middle school.

The boy was quick and agile, but he was still so small. There were a million things he could get into and not have the height or weight to get out of. Alex felt as though he'd aged a year for every hour Jerrod had been missing. He pictured Jerrod, when they'd first met. He remembered the look on his face as he bounced that hammer in his hand.

Alex tested the large flashlight.

The reasonable approach to this situation would be to ride the perimeter, and then tighten the circle until he found Jerrod, or God forbid, reached the middle. The wooded areas would be the hardest, but hopefully Jerrod would be able to answer his calls.

As he rode south, he watched for breaks in the fence that might have caused Jerrod to follow stray cattle. The fence was in excellent condition. Jerrod loved his horse too much to expect him to jump bare barbed wire.

Drifter was a good horse. If he'd been spooked and thrown Jerrod, he would have returned to the barn by now. It was past feeding time. Either Jerrod was on that horse's back, or he'd tied him up somewhere.

Alex reached the southeast corner and turned toward the east. He cursed when a few light raindrops dotted the saddle leather between his legs. He hoped his visibility wouldn't be more impaired than it already was. About a mile straight ahead, toward the lake, he thought he saw a flash of light. Was it lightning? He hadn't heard thunder. Thunder and a harder rain would make it more difficult to hear far off voices. Maybe it was just his eyes playing tricks on him. But no, there it was again, the light and no thunder. He kicked Stardust into a faster gait. The raindrops were getting fatter and much more frequent. Where was that boy?

The third time he saw the light, he knew it was coming from the edge of the lake. It had to be Jerrod. He was already riding as hard as he safely could, over unfamiliar ground. He couldn't risk Stardust stepping into a hole and being injured.

As he reined in his horse, a second horse snorted

and stomped. The noise came from a small stand of trees to the right. It was Drifter, Jerrod's horse. Alex tied Stardust to a bush nearby. A small, clear beam of light came from over the bank.

Alex stepped to the edge. Below, the muddy sides had been deeply scored all the way to the water. At the edge, Jerrod looked up from under his beat-up cowboy hat. He was half submerged and shivering. He had a penlight in his left hand. His right arm was wrapped around the neck of a young calf, trying to keep its head from going under.

Alex peeled off his denim button-down, his T-shirt, and his shoes. He emptied his pockets and slid down the mud on his ass like it was a water slide.

"What took you so damned long?" Jerrod asked in a weak voice. His lips had turned blue and his teeth were chattering. "This bull calf has two legs tangled in the grass and roots down below. He was running from me and slid off in the mud. Dumb critter."

Together they were able to untangle the calf and use their saddle ropes to pull him up. The calf bucked and bawled until he reached flat land, and then he went limp. Alex was fairly certain the little bull was in shock. He probably wouldn't have survived much longer. There was still a good chance he'd end up as veal before the week was over.

If there was one bit of good news, it was that the rain had stopped before it had really gotten started.

"I thought you didn't get attached to the livestock," he said.

"I couldn't just waste him." Jerrod shrugged. He tugged off his sodden T-shirt, and then commandeered the denim outer shirt Alex had taken off. "Even with two banged-up legs he's a valuable animal. Do you have any idea how much veal goes for per pound?"

Alex chuckled and shook his head as he dialed Lacey's phone number. There wasn't an ounce of city in that boy.

"Have Jenna call off the search while you bring us a truck. We've got an injured calf, but Jerrod is fine. Just go southeast toward the lake and you'll see our fire."

By the time he'd covered the calf with Drifter's saddle blanket and built a fire, Jerrod had already polished off half the food he'd brought and drank a full bottle of water.

As they waited, Alex rubbed the calf's body to get him warmed up. He wasn't about to let him die on the ground. Not after all Jerrod had been through to keep him.

Jerrod stared into the fire and rubbed his hands together. "I helped Mom birth that calf," he said. "It was my first. I couldn't believe his mother was able to get up and walk after all that. She took to the little guy like nothing had ever happened. How do you suppose a female can do something like that?"

"It's just nature, I guess." Alex wished the boy had asked about football. "Females have a way of getting past the bad parts fast so that they can get on with the nurturing. It's one of those mysteries of life."

"I guess that's how they get over the mating part too." Jerrod broke a stick into little pieces and fed each one into the fire. "I don't know if I could put a woman through either experience."

Alex leaned forward and studied the boy. Was he saying what he thought he was? "What makes you say a thing like that?"

"You'll probably just think I'm weird or something."

"Of course I won't."

Jerrod threw the rest of the stick into the fire and wiped his hands on his thighs. "A few months back, I was working on a fence. I was taking a break in the truck when one of the bulls mounted a female. It was kind of scary to watch, but I'd never been out here to see that before. I couldn't look away."

"That's okay," Alex assured him.

"Well, she got all crazy with fear and bawled and fought, but the bull wouldn't leave her alone. He looked like the devil, biting and bucking at her until I thought he'd kill her. Of course I stayed in the truck. I knew I couldn't stop him. When he was done, he just walked off. I had a mind to shoot that bull."

Alex smiled to himself. The boy probably didn't have a rifle handy or he'd have done it. How long had he had this on his mind?

"Well, Jerrod, that's one of the things that make most men different than animals. Its men like us that have to protect women from the other kind of men."

Jerrod looked Alex in the eyes. "I'd kill a man who treated a woman that way. Especially if it was my mom or Jenna he was after."

Is that why Jerrod had given him such a hard time about getting close to Lacey? Was he afraid he'd hurt her?

"I'm glad to hear that. You just say the word and I'll have your back. I'd never let any harm come to them either."

Jerrod took the last biscuit in the bag and nibbled

on it. "So, what makes a woman want to be with a man?"

Just when he thought this conversation was over, damn.

"Like I said, it's different with people. They start out as friends. If they're lucky, they start falling in love. If the other person loves them back, they know they can trust each other. Sometimes they find out they aren't meant to stay together, but when they do find that one special person that was made just for them, no one else will do."

"Have you ever found that one special person?" Jerrod asked.

"I'm pretty sure I have," Alex said with a smile.

"What makes it different?"

Will this inquisition never end?

"I guess it's the love that makes the biggest difference. Respecting what she does and the way she feels about things, even if you don't understand it sometimes. Making her happy is the only thing that makes you happy. Being willing to kill or die to keep her safe. And, the most important thing is letting her know she's loved, always treating her tenderly. When you have all that, making love is beautiful for both of you. It's a more emotional process for humans, or at least it should be."

Jerrod nodded his head and stared into the fire in quiet contemplation.

Alex had given himself a lot to think about as well.

****

Lacey flew out of her truck and ran to her son so fast she wasn't sure if her feet had touched the ground. He looked so small in Alex's shirt. Her hands shook as she brushed the hair off his forehead. She wanted to look into his eyes. She could always tell everything about him that way. If he was sick, hurt, upset, or angry, it was always right there in those expressive, jade green eyes.

What she saw now was soft, patient, indulgence. He stepped forward and wrapped his arms around her, gently patting her back. He'd known that's what she needed. Dammit, why did he have to grow up so fast?

"I'm all right, Mom, just real tired. I need to get Drifter back home and taken care of."

"Don't worry about Drifter." Lacey reluctantly drew back. "You'll need to ride with the calf. I don't want him sliding around in the back of the truck. Alex will help me take care of the horses. I've got two pieces of chocolate cake and tall glasses of milk with you guys' names on them, at the house."

"It's not the weekend," Jerrod said with wide eyes. "Where did you get a chocolate cake?"

"I was nervous and had nothing to do so I baked a cake. So sue me."

"I'm sorry I made you nervous, Mom," Jerrod said. "I just couldn't let that calf drown."

"I know," Lacey said, hoping there wouldn't be another scare like this again.

Jenna had stayed quiet as she'd put out the small campfire and led Drifter away from the trees. She flung his stirrup over the saddle to tighten his cinch.

Lacey knew what she was thinking. She'd watched Alex lift the calf into the bed of her truck. He was still beside her, so it was his arm she gripped, when she thought of her second child riding so late at night. Thankfully, Alex intervened.

"Leave him be, Jenna," he said. "That horse isn't taking a rider tonight. He hasn't had food or water since about noon."

"I'll ride double with you then," Jenna replied stubbornly.

"No you won't." Alex sounded as stern as…as a father. "I'll be leading Drifter slowly. Your mom may need help before I get back."

"But I want to stay with you," Jenna whined.

"I said no. Now get your skinny behind in that truck before I decide to paddle it."

When Jenna walked past her mom, she gave her a secret little wink and a grin.

Chapter Twenty-One

The timer buzzed on the oven to let Lacey know the cornbread was ready to come out. It was Friday evening and Alex would arrive soon.

So much had happened since she'd walked into Alex's Orlando office. They'd made an agreement to be married in a month. The month had come and gone. Their marriage license had expired.

Alex had mentioned marriage a few times, but she'd resisted the idea. Then she ran into Donna Sullivan in his house. It seemed obvious he'd changed his mind. Surely he didn't expect her to make a commitment to him when he was seeing another woman. Was he still so angry with her that he'd expect the marriage to be one-sided? He'd been so casual about the incident.

It was best she hadn't told the kids about their plan. She was sure it wouldn't happen now.

However, Alex still seemed to be blending into their lives as though he'd always been there. Jenna was crazy about him, for good reason. She couldn't wait for him to step into the role of father. Now, Jerrod was coming around as well. Alex was becoming the hero to them that she'd thought he was when she was young.

He wasn't a boy anymore. He'd become more of a man than she'd ever dreamed he'd be. But his armor had tarnished in her mind, when she'd left his house the last time.

At the table, Jenna had a meat fork in each hand, quietly pulling a pork roast. She'd become more content since she'd realized the truth, but she was anxious and impatient about Alex's reaction to the news of his fatherhood. Somehow, she'd have to find the right time, place, and courage to tell him. And it had to be soon, maybe tonight.

The sound of a large truck motor came from the gravel drive. It was too late for a delivery. Lacey couldn't imagine who it could be. She turned the oven off and walked to the front door with Jenna curiously crowding her from behind.

In front of the house, a full sized, brand new, crew-cab pickup truck sat idling. Attached to its tow hitch was a top-of-the-line horse trailer. It could easily carry four animals. Both were painted a light brown color that reminded her of sand after a wave of salt water had washed over it. What awed Lacey most was that both had the Double J brand emblazoned on their sides.

Alex stepped from the driver's seat. He turned his old straw cowboy hat in his hands, as though he was nervous. That hat and his boots looked well-worn, but the sunglasses must've cost a couple hundred dollars.

"Do you like the color?" he asked. "It was the hardest part to decide on. I figured if I went too dark, it would absorb heat. A light color would show dirt before you could reach the road. And, I was afraid anything too bright might attract unwanted attention from the bulls. But if you don't like it, I can have it repainted any color you like."

Was he serious? Buck curiously sniffed the tires of the new trailer and she hoped he wouldn't lift his leg.

"Alex, I don't care what color they are." A dull ache was settling at the front of her head. As badly as she'd like to, she couldn't give in to *want*. "This farm can't afford a new truck and trailer."

"Hey, what's the idea?" Jerrod's voice came from the direction of the barn. "How come you're using our brand?"

"When I left here Wednesday night, I couldn't sleep," Alex explained. "I got on the internet and, well, I bought a truck and trailer."

"Just like that?" Jerrod exclaimed. "You just up and bought 'em?"

"Hold on Mr. Moneybags." The pain in her head was escalating. In another minute her eyes would pop out of their sockets. "If these are assets of the farm, the farm has to pay for them. We can't do that."

"Yes you can," Alex insisted. "I added enough capital in the farm to cover them easily."

"What do you mean you added capital?" Jerrod was stunned. "You may own the dirt under our feet, but these are our crops and livestock. You can't just come in and take over."

"I'm not taking over." Alex rolled his eyes and huffed. "It's like a partnership. Neither one of us-meaning your mom or me, Mr. Buttinski-can run this farm without the other. I own the land and buildings. She owns everything else, including the know-how. I think we could make this place pay off better by putting a little more into it."

"Yeah, sure," Jerrod grumbled. "Just what I need, more to take care of."

"Well that's another thing," Alex began.

"What's Jenna doing with that guy?" Jerrod

interrupted.

Turning to see what Jerrod was talking about, Lacey saw Jenna at the back of the now opened trailer with a handsome young cowboy. He was leading a chestnut gelding down the ramp.

"What's this?" she asked, indicating the horse.

"This is Mercury. He's mine as of this morning." Alex smiled proudly as he approached the animal and smoothed his hand down the deep red neck. "After riding Stardust, I got an urge to have my own horse. I remembered that a friend of mine had Mercury up for sale. I used to ride him when I visited his ranch outside of Orlando. What do you think?"

"I think he's magnificent." Lacey inspected every inch of the horse. The beautiful gelding caused her headache to ease. Mercury was solid with a strong back and a proud stance. Despite the long ride he'd taken in a strange trailer, he was remarkably calm and well mannered. He'd been cared for and trained well.

Jerrod took his lead rope and started toward the barn. "He looks like a hay burning, manure machine to me," he grumbled.

"Where do you want this, Mr. Benson?" The young cowboy held a black tooled saddle with silver studs.

The boy was about seventeen, had shaggy blond hair, and was built like Alex had been at that age. Clearly, he was no stranger to animals or the outdoors.

"Jenna will show you as soon as you say hello to Ms. Carlyle. You'll be taking most of your orders from her. She runs the place." Alex turned his smile her way. "Lacey, this is Darrel Taylor. He and his brother Ben are going to help you out, a few days a week. We'll work out the specifics over supper."

Before Lacey had a chance to question this second decision Alex had made without her, an older truck rolled up the drive.

The driver, Ben Taylor, looked a lot like Darrel, but a couple of years older. His manner was more reserved and his hair was neater. He explained that their grandmother was waiting supper for them. They were soon gone.

"I found Darrel and Ben at the feed store looking for work," Alex said, as they walked toward the house. "They're a little hard up for money. I'll pay their wages myself until we increase the herd and start making a better profit."

"Well, thanks for letting me know." Lacey wasn't ashamed of the sarcasm that dripped from her words. "An expensive truck and trailer, another horse, two new farmhands, and now a larger herd-the hits just keep coming."

"Exactly what is the problem?" Alex stopped to block her way. "I'm trying to help you make the farm more profitable. I'm trying to make your life easier. I'd hoped this would be the *more* you wanted. I don't get the attitude."

"I started this farm with my own two hands." Lacey laid her fist against her chest. "I'm the one that burned the brand into that sign above the gate. I've poured my blood, sweat and tears into this place for eight years. I understand that you own this land now, but I'd at least like a say in what goes on here."

For several seconds, Alex stared at her with tight lips. "I just wanted to be a part of things. Maybe I got a little carried away." He slapped his hat against the thigh of his relaxed fit jeans. "I'm not a control freak. I'm just used to being in charge. I haven't had to share anything since Travis and I slept in the same room."

"I guess we've both got things to work on," Lacey conceded.

Jerrod exploded from the barn and stomped past them. "All the damnable changes around this place, extra people and animals to deal with, now Jenna's moonin' over that blond haired cowboy. My life is going to hell in a hand basket."

"You know," Alex mused, "that boy takes a lot after your granddad." Buck snorted as he walked a slow circle around them. "For that matter, so does your dog."

****

Over supper, the four of them discussed what chores the Taylor boys would take over. The conversation became livelier when the kids realized that they'd have more time to do things away from the farm. They suggested everything from a beach trip to a cruise to Alaska. They were all in a much better mood when banana cream pie was served.

Alex was relieved that the tension had eased. "Now that supper is over, I have a surprise for everyone."

He walked out to the new truck and came back with a shopping bag. Inside were three boxes, all the same size and shape, but wrapped in different colored paper.

Alex was excited to see their reactions to his gifts, but they didn't open them or even seem curious. Lacey stared at the box in her hand while the kids stared at her.

"What did I do now?" Alex asked.

"Are you one of those weirdoes who celebrate Christmas in July?" Jerrod responded.

"You don't have to give us things," Jenna said. "We like you just...because."

"I know it's not Christmas, dammit, and I'm not trying to buy your affection." Totally perplexed, Alex stated, "I don't know how to relate to you people. Why does one small gesture have to be such a big deal? Just open the damned things."

When Jenna tore the first piece of paper from her gift, Jerrod decided to follow her lead. They each uncovered new cell phones, Jenna's in red and Jerrod's in blue. The fact that they just stared at them with opened mouths made Alex even more uncomfortable. Lacey unwrapped hers to find a silver phone.

"Each of our numbers is already programmed into all the phones and they're operational, they've even been charged. Of course, I'm sure your mom will have a few rules regarding their use."

"Alex," Lacey cried, "this is too much. We can't accept these. We don't need them."

Alex ran his hands down his face to hold back his growing annoyance. "I don't know anyone who needs them more. Look at what's happened around here recently. When Jerrod fell through the porch floor, when Jenna got sick at a friend's house, it could have happened anywhere. There's a chance that next time, we'd have to call 911. Do you realize how much faster we could have gotten to Jerrod when he was struggling with that calf in the lake? We're lucky they didn't both drown. I was able to call you when I found him because I had a phone in my pocket. These are all on the same plan I already have. Think of them as farm equipment, just the same as the truck or the tools. Businesses everywhere use them. Why can't you just enjoy them?"

"Hey," Jerrod exclaimed, "this thing gets internet."

"We aren't used to so much extravagance, Alex." Lacey set the box on the table, as though she was afraid it would break. "We don't have much, but we get by."

"I don't want you to get by," Alex bellowed. "I want to make your lives better. Why can't these kids have the things that other kids all over the country enjoy-hell, take for granted?"

"They aren't like other kids," Lacey shot back. "I'm trying to raise them with good values. I don't want them to be like the spoiled brats they see on TV. Not everything can be made better by throwing money at it."

"These are good kids, smart kids. They work hard. They deserve a few basic conveniences." He'd succeeded in calming his voice if nothing else. "If it seems like I'm throwing money around, maybe it's because there is so much to catch up on around here. I'm not taking a damned bit of it back. You should learn to accept things more graciously and take a step into the twenty-first century. Dammit, you tell me you want more, but when I try to give you things, it's still not enough."

"Oh, look," Jenna squealed. "I just sent a text to Jerrod."

"When I said that, Alex, I didn't mean I wanted your money. I'm not a gold-digger. We did just fine before you came here." Lacey leveled narrowed eyes on him. "And, we'll do just fine after you leave."

"I'm not going anywhere. I'm a permanent part of this farm now, so get used to it."

"Does that mean I'll also have to get used to Donna Sullivan?" Lacey's question shot out like a poisoned dart.

"What does my receptionist have to do with anything? She works for East Coast L.D., not the Double J." Alex stood and took his plate to the sink. "I'll unhitch the trailer so you can give me a ride home."

****

Lacey turned the key in the big, new truck and felt the powerful engine catch on the first try. The rumble, though barely audible, sent a thrill through her body. It was a nice truck. And how many times had she wished for her own trailer?

She'd given up on wishes a long time ago, but now, it seemed that Alex was making a few of them come true.

Her biggest wish was for him to come home, and here he was.

Why was she being so contrary? Would it be so bad to try to trust him one more time?

She pulled out onto the highway. Several times in the first few miles, she looked over to the passenger side. He sat slumped in the seat with his legs stretched out and his head against the window. He nervously bit a fingernail as he watched the landscape pass. Lacey made her decision.

She pulled into the side road that lead to the old clearing and stopped. Their special spot was only a few yards away, but the truck was too big to pass through the overgrown path.

Alex slid up straighter in his seat and looked around. "What are we doing here?"

"I've been meaning to look around and see what would have to be done to clean this place up. Don't you think it would make a nice picnic spot?"

"Oh," he mumbled. "I guess so."

Was that a look of disappointment? Lacey opened her door and stepped to the ground. "As long as we're here," she pulled her shirt over her head and tossed it to him, "there's something I've been dying to do."

Alex's face lit up. "I'm right behind you, sweetheart." As the buttons gave way on his own shirt he ran behind her to their private haven.

It had been difficult for Alex at first. He'd wanted to keep Lacey turned away from him, but she'd have none of that. She stopped, stood and turned here side to him, naked as the day she was born.

"Can you see all the little stretch marks on my hips and under my belly?" She grazed her fingers over her hips up her sides.

"Yes. What does it matter? They're your little badges of courage. I intend to lick every one of them at some point tonight."

"You aren't repulsed by them?"

"No, of course not." He smiled wickedly and knelt in the grass. "Standing there, like a pagan goddess, you're just making me want you more."

She turned toward him. "My hips are wider. My breasts and belly are softer." Her fingers traveled gracefully under her breasts and continued up to lift her hair off her neck.

Alex rose up on his knees as if to beg. "You're killing me, woman," he groaned.

Lacey lifted a finger and turned it in the air. "Turn around."

"You don't want to see that, Lacey." Misery etched his face.

"I showed you mine, now you show me yours. No more secrets. No more hiding."

He slowly obeyed. Still kneeling, he turned his back to her. She wanted to cry when she saw the scars that sectioned and marbled the left side of his back, but she wouldn't allow herself to do that to him.

His hands were clutched behind his head and his shoulders were slumped forward like he was waiting to be beaten. She'd never seen such a frightened gesture from such a brave man. It had been hard for him to do as she'd asked, exposing his greatest insecurity. She wanted to show him that he'd never have to hide anything from her again.

He caught his breath as her lips moved gently over his shoulders and down his back. Dampness glistened in his eyes as his hands relaxed and he turned to her.

They both knew it wasn't their first time, but their encounter was better earned this time. They'd both been through hell and had come out on the other side.

Maturity had taught them to appreciate the little things-the texture and taste, the scent and sight of each other, the sound of their name from the other's cries of ecstasy. Under a full moon, over soft grass, they became one again.

****

Three hours later, Lacey snuck into her quiet house and took a warm shower. She changed into her nightgown and brushed her hair.

Her new cell phone had been left on her dresser. She picked up the small gadget to inspect it. When it rang for the first time, she nearly dropped it. It rang twice more before she figured out how to open it.

"Hello?"

"I just wanted to tell you that supper, and everything, was wonderful tonight, thank you."

"I enjoyed it too," she replied.

"Good night, Lacey."

"Good night."

Chapter Twenty-Two

Alex was coming through his back door after his Saturday morning run. A long cool shower and a glass of iced coffee were his only other plans for the morning, until his cell phone rang. He mopped the sweat from his face with a dishtowel, and then tossed it in the general direction of the laundry room. He could always let the call go to voice mail, but what if it was another Double J disaster? He was quickly learning that anything could happen at the farm at any given time. He'd never let Lacey hear him say it, but he wondered how they'd survived so far.

"Hello?"

"Hey, Alex. I was wondering, how much money do you have?"

Alex hadn't thought to check the caller ID, but he recognized Jerrod's voice immediately. "I couldn't say right offhand, but I could put you in touch with my accountant, if it's important to you."

"You're a funny guy, Alex. What I meant was, do you have any cash on you?"

"I keep a few bucks around. Why do you ask?" Alex replied.

"I'm tapped and I didn't want to ask Mom for ten bucks. She thinks I'm in town to skateboard, but I want to do something she doesn't know about."

"I so hope you're not asking me to be an accessory

to a crime."

"No, I just wanted to do something on my own. She'll be surprised, but she's not going to shoot me or anything."

"Okay, what do you have in mind?"

"I want to get a haircut, a real one. These curls are too girlish and they're hell to deal with, out in the heat."

Alex scratched his chin. "You know, I feel the same way about this beard and I could use a trim. Let me jump through the shower, and then I'll meet you at Westin's Barber Shop. Give me twenty minutes."

Jerrod was pacing the sidewalk, looking as nervous as a long-tailed cat in a rocking chair factory. Alex was willing to bet that the only haircuts he'd ever had were done with his mom's sewing scissors. Women didn't understand the anxiety a boy could have about his appearance. A boy Jerrod's age didn't bitch about his hair. That would be much too wimpy. But he was ready to start making a good impression for the ladies. This new concern may have been spurred on by Jenna's attraction to the Taylor boy following on the coattails of Lacey's and his new relationship. He'd just have to teach the kid how to cowboy-up a bit.

"I don't really know what to ask for in there." Jerrod lamented. "You don't think they'll do something weird to me do you?"

Alex ruffled the boy's curly mop of hair for the last time. "Don't worry, kid. The Westin brothers were the only ones to touch my curly locks until the Navy got hold of me. Now if you want to talk about bad haircuts, you should have seen me then. I'll handle this."

"I'm not going to have to wear hair gel, am I?" Jerrod was actually sweating.

"I wouldn't recommend it. To be honest, it's an itchy, sticky mess under a hat in the afternoon sun." Alex opened the door and led Jerrod inside.

"As I live and breathe." Carl Westin grinned. "It's Alex Benson, all grown up. I'm not going to have to bribe you with a lollipop this time, am I?"

"That happened one time when I was three-years-old, Mr. Westin," Alex reminded him. "I found out that lollipops and flying hair clippings don't make a good mix. You can trim the sides and back close, but leave it a bit longer on top. About an inch and a half would be good. Use scissors, not clippers. I'd also like to get rid of this beard." He turned to Lloyd Westin. "Give my buddy, Jerrod, the same, minus the shave."

They each sat in chairs and had nylon capes snapped out and placed around their necks.

"You sure you don't want me to buzz this boy bald, like some of them rap singers do?" Lloyd chuckled.

Jerrod had a look of shear panic in his eyes.

"Not unless you plan to clean up more than hair under that chair," Alex told the barber.

Carl Westin leaned Alex's chair back and placed a hot, damp towel over his face to soften his beard. After a few minutes, the bell over the door jingled.

"Hey there, Sport," the newcomer said. "Are you going to be ready to be on my team this year?"

That scratchy voice seemed familiar.

"I've been practicing all year, Mr. Walker," Jerrod said.

Alex peeked out from under a corner of the towel. An old high school buddy of his stood beside Jerrod. He pulled the towel off and hung it over the arm of the chair. "Nate Walker, how are you doing, man?" They shook hands. "I didn't know Jerrod played sports. What do you coach?"

"Mr. Walker teaches calf roping for the junior rodeo," Jerrod answered instead. "In December, I'll be old enough for the advanced competition."

"It's hard to believe so much time has gone by since the year these kids were born," Lloyd Westin recalled. "That was the worse Christmas the people in this town can remember. We thought we were going to lose them all. That Lacey Carlyle is one strong woman."

Nate Walker cleared his throat loudly and gave Lloyd a stern look.

"No need to talk about such things in front of the boy," Carl Westin whispered to his brother. He had Alex's face smoothly shaved with a few swipes of his straight razor. "We just count our blessings and move on."

"Well," Nate said, "we'll be starting practice next month. I know I should wait until Jerrod turns thirteen, but the competitions begin in January. Truth be told, he's probably ready now, anyway."

Alex leaned his head forward while Carl made short work with his scissors.

Nate must have made a mistake. Jared couldn't be thirteen in December. That would place his birth only five months after he'd left for the Navy. He'd taken Lacey's virginity the month before that…hadn't he? He was only eighteen at the time. Could he have been that naïve?

He'd calculated the dates several times over the last month. If the twins were his they wouldn't be thirteen until March or April of next year.

Was it possible that Lacey had already been pregnant their first time together? She would have told him, wouldn't she? Could that be why she'd never tried to find him?

No, the kids were too small to be thirteen. But he didn't really know much about kids. Jerrod had told him he was the smallest kid in his class, just like he'd been.

She hadn't looked pregnant. She didn't even have a boyfriend back then. Could something have happened to her? How could he just come out and ask her a thing like that? She might be hiding something she's ashamed of, something too hard to talk about.

She'd told the kids that their father was her one true love. Had she lied to spare them an ugly truth?

It was time to get to the bottom of this, once and for all.

Carl Westin wiped the remnants of shaving cream off Alex's ears and removed the cape. Lastly, he brushed the loose hair clippings from his neck.

"There you go, Jerrod." Lloyd had gone through the same routine at the other chair. "How do you like it?"

"I like it fine," Jerrod said. "What do you think, Alex?"

Alex nodded without really looking. "It's fine. Grab your skateboard and I'll take you home. I've got business to discuss with your mother."

Alex pulled a fifty-dollar bill from the wad of money in his pocket and handed it to Carl.

"You only owe us thirty bucks for both haircuts and the shave."

"Split the change." Alex was already through the

door.

Jerrod did as he was told, wondering what he'd done this time. Alex was obviously bent out of shape about something.

Once they'd left town, Alex finally spoke. "You were born on Christmas?"

"Christmas Eve," Jerrod answered.

"Exactly how old are you right now?"

"Well, I don't have a calculator, but I'll be thirteen in five months, give or take a few days, hours, and minutes."

The rest of the ride was silent and tense.

Chapter Twenty-Three

Lacey was doing paperwork when the screen door slammed. She recognized the heavy, rapid footfalls going up the stairs. Jerrod was home and he was upset about something. His bedroom door slammed.

"Jerrod, is everything all right?" she called from the foot of the stairs.

When there was no answer she walked up a few steps. "Jerrod, come down here right now. I want to know what's going on."

"I do too, Mom," Jerrod replied through his closed door. "But I'm not coming out of this room until the first snowfall."

"For heaven's sake, this is Florida. You've never seen snow." Lacey climbed the rest of the way up the stairs. "How'd you get home from town? You were supposed to call when you were ready to be picked up. I didn't hear a car pull in."

"Alex's BMW is a lot quieter than the old trucks around here."

"Alex is here, now, why? What happened?" she was getting frustrated, hollering at a closed door.

"I don't know," Jerrod bellowed. "I'm just tired of the grown-ups around here acting so weird. Alex is mad about something and I didn't do anything."

"Well, what did he say?"

"Nothing, he just got all weird and asked me about

my birthday and stuff."

Lacey's heart leapt into her throat. It was too late to break it to him gently. He'd found out on his own. No doubt, he was furious.

"I think I know what the problem is. I'll take care of it. We'll all sit down and talk about it in a little while. Just come out of there."

"Nope, I've had enough."

Lacey had had enough too. "Jerrod, if you don't open this door, I swear I'll take it off the hinges."

The door swung open, revealing a red faced, short-haired Jerrod. "It's not locked," Jerrod shouted.

Lacey threw her hands up to cover her gasp. "What did you do?" Then she looked at him closer and smiled. "I like it, it looks nice."

"Forget the hair. I want to know what I did wrong."

"It's nothing you did. I'm the one in trouble this time." When Jerrod's lips tightened and his eyes narrowed, she added, "Everything is going to be fine. Alex and I just need some time to talk about a few things."

****

"What a wonderful surprise!" Cheryl Benson exclaimed through the receiver of Alex's cell phone. "Your father is going to be so disappointed he wasn't here to say hello. We've tried to call, but your home phones been disconnected and it seems your office has moved."

"Yes, Mother, I know. I moved with it. You should have tried my cell phone."

"Oh, I couldn't do that." She gasped. "Those things are so expensive. Where did you move to, darling? I hope it's not too far away."

"I moved back to Indian Lakes."

"What in the world for? It's such a tiny little town, no culture, no ambiance."

"It was good enough when we were growing up," Alex replied. "I have a great house in the middle of town and I've already run into a lot of old friends."

"Oh, how nice, anyone I'd remember?"

"Maybe. Do you remember Lacey Carlyle?"

"Oh dear, I hope you're not going to get involved with that girl again. She almost trapped you into marriage when you weren't even out of your teens."

"What do you mean, Mom?" Alex probed.

"Honey, a mother knows things. I knew when you started getting serious about that girl. You stopped hanging out with your friends. It only took a month for her to talk you into dropping your scholarship and joining the Navy. And then you were only gone ten weeks when she showed up asking about you. Her belly was so big with a baby and I knew it couldn't be yours. I told her right then and there, that you deserved better than her. Thank goodness she never came back."

What Lacey had told him was true. His mother had turned her away. He felt sick. When he glanced toward the house, he saw Lacey approaching.

"Something's just come up. I have to go. Tell the family I said hello. I'll see you soon."

"I love you, Son." Cheryl sounded desperate, as though she'd never hear from him again.

"I love you too, Mom." The words caught in his throat. Alex had never been ashamed of his mother until now. She'd been no better than the other women in this town. She'd turned away the orphaned daughter of her best friend at a time when she needed help the most. He was afraid he would say something very ugly if he stayed on the line a moment longer.

****

With every step she took, Lacey's nervousness grew until she felt like she'd be sick, but she refused to give in to it. It was past time to clear the air. She didn't have a clue what to say, how to begin. But then she didn't have to. Alex spoke first.

"I would have stayed. I would have found a way to make things right, if you had just told me." His voice was so low she could barely hear him.

"I didn't know," she murmured.

"How could you not know, Lacey? You're smarter than that." Alex gripped her shoulders. "Were you afraid of what I'd think? I would have understood. We could have worked it out. Sure, I'd have been upset, but I would have helped you out."

"Helped me out?" Lacey was confused. "You make it sound like it was all my doing."

"I do know about the birds and the bees. I know you weren't alone in this, but that wouldn't have mattered." Alex pulled her closer. "However it happened, whoever you'd been with, you could have come to me."

"What are you saying?" Lacey didn't get a chance to finish before hell broke loose once again.

A scream, hollering, running, and bellowing neighs, something had happened in the pens. A horse was in distress.

The scene, as she raced toward it, made her blood freeze in her veins and her heart clench painfully. Buttercup was in the barrel pen lying on her side. She kicked her powerful legs to gain purchase, trying to stand. Jenna was pinned under her heavy body. She wasn't moving.

Jerrod pulled at Buttercup's harness to lift her head. Darrell squatted by Jenna, pushing at the horse's hindquarter. Ben knelt at Jenna's head, holding each side of her face. He had blood on his hands. The horse finally rose to her feet, but Jenna still didn't move or make a sound.

Alex grabbed two large blocks of wood from beside the gate and placed them at each side of Jenna's head to relieve Ben from his position.

"Did you move her?" he asked.

"I know better than that," Ben replied.

Alex pulled his cell phone from his pocket and dialed 911.

"You'd better see to Buttercup, Ben." Lacey knelt by her daughter. "She may be injured as well."

"I'll see to Buttercup from the business end of a shotgun," Jerrod snapped.

"This wasn't her fault," Ben insisted. "Jenna was taking those barrels like a bat out of hell."

"Jenna was racing barrels?" Lacey cried. "She's not trained for that. Buttercup isn't even trained for the barrels. I told Jenna she had to wait until she was older."

"It's my fault," Darrell admitted. "I was telling her earlier how cool it was when I watched you do it."

"I may be to blame too," Jerrod added. "I've been bragging about training for the junior rodeo. I knew she wanted to compete in the barrels."

By the time Jenna was placed on the ambulance gurney, she'd regained consciousness. Alex watched the doors close her and Lacey inside and pull away, sirens screaming and lights flashing.

"Ben, I'd appreciate it if one of you boys stayed to watch the house and finish up around here until we get back."

"No problem, Boss."

Jerrod was already in the passenger seat of the BMW when Alex got in.

Chapter Twenty-Four

Her children had been sick and injured several times throughout their childhoods, but never had they been through the emergency room. They'd certainly never ridden in the back of an ambulance. Not since the day they were born.

Lacey had been left standing at the entrance. They'd said it was too crowded and hectic in the examination room. Wasn't it just as bad for the people in charge of her daughter's life? Why weren't the rooms larger? Why wasn't the medical team more efficient?

They'd said they might have to give Jenna tests that she couldn't be present at. The radiation exposure would be dangerous. If it was too dangerous for Lacey to be near, how dangerous was it for her child?

Everything had happened in rapid-fire motion since she'd heard Jenna scream. But now, waiting from outside the treatment rooms, time stood still.

Lacey wrapped her arms around herself because she didn't have anything stronger to hold on to. She paced the floor with no place to go, but if she stopped for a single moment, she'd scream, and she might not be able to stop.

She always knew that farming, cattle, and horses were dangerous, but that's the life she'd raised her kids in. She'd put them at risk and this was the pay-off.

Maybe her grandfather had been right all along.

The sliding doors swooshed open. Alex ran toward her with Jerrod by his side. The anxiety on their faces matched the aching in her heart.

"Have you heard anything?" Alex asked.

"Not a word. I don't know what's going on and they won't let me go back there." Those few words were all it took to start the tears that had been waiting. Alex and Jerrod hugged her from each side. Now, she had something strong to hold on to and she could finally stop.

"What's going on here?" Clarence bellowed from the doorway. "Bob Johnson, from the office here, called and said my granddaughter had been brought in by ambulance. Why didn't you call me?"

"She fell from her horse," Jerrod told him. "But it didn't occur to us that you'd care."

"Jerrod don't," Lacey said weakly.

"I expected something like this to happen," Clarence declared.

"You should. Kids have accidents all the time. Especially active kids like these. If you even think about blaming Lacey for this," Alex threatened, "I'll take you outside and make you part of the pavement."

"Please Alex," Lacey begged. "We don't need any more drama today."

"Ms. Carlyle," a lady at the desk called. "We need to get some information from you. If you'll step over here, we'll get started on the paperwork."

"I'll go with you," Alex said.

"I'll take the boy and find some coffee." Clarence clamped his hand on Jerrod's shoulder to lead him away.

"The boy's name is Jerrod. Try using it once in a while," Jerrod sneered.

Lacey would have to talk to Jerrod about showing his great-grandfather more respect, but healing the rift their last meeting had caused was going to take time. Right now, she had bigger problems.

"I didn't bring my purse," she told the woman straight out. The nameplate on her desk identified her as Jan Holcomb. "I was more concerned about my daughter. Even if I had, I don't have any insurance."

"Well, that'll just take a little extra paperwork and we'll see if we can get the county to help out." Jan smiled.

"No need," Alex interrupted. "I'll take care of the bill."

"Alex, you can't do that."

"Yes I can. It's not a problem. I don't want you to worry about money right now. Jenna is enough to worry about." He turned to the woman. "Just show me where to sign."

After entering the information Lacey provided, Jan looked at her computer and gasped. "Is this the same Jenna Carlyle that was brought in thirteen years ago with her twin brother?"

"That was twelve and a half years ago," Lacey corrected. She glanced nervously at Alex and added, "The day they were born."

"Oh my," Jan's fingers flew over her keyboard faster. "We'll have to search the database for a donor right away, just in case we need someone."

"Donor, what the hell are you talking about?" Alex looked at Lacey. "What's wrong?"

"Jenna has a rare blood type." Lacey hadn't

considered that problem. Her panic built again.

"A hospital this size doesn't have AB negative blood on hand," Jan added. "We rarely have need of it. Jenna and her brother are rarer because their blood lacks an antigen that most others have."

Alex slumped back in his chair looking stunned. "I'm a rare blood donor." He pulled a Red Cross card from his wallet and handed it to Jan. "Am I a match?"

Jan carefully compared the card to her computer screen. "This is wonderful," Jan exclaimed. "I'll call an orderly so that we can start processing right away. What an incredible coincidence."

"Yes, isn't it?" he quipped as he glared at Lacey.

****

An hour later, Alex entered the waiting room where Jerrod and Clarence were thumbing through magazines. Empty coffee cups littered the table in front of them.

"I got you a cup of coffee," Clarence groused. "Jerrod drank it."

"They said you were going to be a while," Jerrod defended himself.

"It doesn't matter." Alex worked with the button on his shirt sleeve. "I just had a bottle of juice. Where's Lacey? Have you heard anything?"

"Mom's back there with Jenna. The doctor says she's going to be okay. She's all bruised up and she has a minor concussion. She'll be able to come home in a couple of days."

"Oh to be young again," Clarence mused. "A fall like that would have killed me."

"We're just waiting around to see her," Jerrod added.

"While we wait, your grandfather can tell us a story." Alex settled into a chair across from Clarence. "Why don't you tell us all about how the twins were born? You know that story, don't you?"

Clarence quickly glanced at Jerrod. "I'm not going to talk about that in front of a child."

"Jerrod isn't a child. He's a half grown man. He works harder than you ever have, he's stronger than you've ever been, and he deserves the truth. So do I."

Clarence made a show of opening another magazine, stubbornly ignoring Alex.

"You've got two choices, old man," Alex snarled. "You can either tell the story, or you can prepare yourself to be wheeled into the next available treatment room with a broken neck."

"Dammit, okay. It wasn't long after you left that I found out Lacey was pregnant. She was sleeping all the time and when she was awake, she was getting sick. I've got to tell you, I was pretty mad. She was too young to have a baby. I figured if I could keep her away from you, she'd give the child up for adoption or something, so I hid your letters. When Lacey started growing so big, the doctor checked her out and found that she was carrying twins. It became harder for her to get around, but she was still young and restless. By the time cold weather set in, she was told to stay off her feet. She'd sit in her room and sew little gowns and knit booties and such. She was disappointed that I wouldn't let her decorate the Christmas tree."

Alex looked over to see Jerrod staring at him slack jawed. It hadn't occurred to him that Alex could be his father. He reached over and squeezed the boy's hand. He hoped he was doing the right thing. "Go on."

"Well, Christmas Eve came around. I went out to run a few last-minute errands. The church wanted a truckload of pine boughs for their pageant scene. I ended up staying longer then I'd expected to help put the thing together. I stopped at the store on my way home to buy a necklace for Lacey's Christmas present. I even had it wrapped.

Lacey waited for me to leave, then came downstairs to put my present under the tree. She'd knitted me a scarf and hat. I've still got them. You remember, I said she wasn't getting around too good. She fell all the way down those stairs. She had a concussion. It probably knocked her out for a while. Both her legs were broken and one hip dislocated. The damage done to her insides caused her to have an emergency hysterectomy. It nearly killed her. She'd just about bled out by the time I found her. There was so much blood."

"Jesus H Christ." Bile burned the back of his throat.

Jerrod's eyes were filling with tears, but Clarence didn't notice. His mind was locked on the past. "The twins were no bigger than newborn kittens, sounded like 'em too. I didn't believe they'd make it, but they were strong. The ambulance attendants said it was a miracle. They were a little more than three months early, but they were already fighters. I guess Lacey is a fighter too, giving birth to twins in that condition and all alone."

Clarence looked around him as though he'd just woken in a strange place. His eyes locked on Jerrod. He frowned when he saw a tear streak down his cheek. "I hope you appreciate all your mother has been through for you kids, Jerrod."

Alex stood and urged Jerrod to his feet. "We're going to take a little walk. If Lacey comes back, tell her we're outside."

Chapter Twenty-Five

"I hate that old man more than fish guts." Jerrod wiped away tears with his sleeve.

"No you don't, Jerrod." Alex walked with him further from the building where they could talk privately. "You hate what he did, so do I. But he truly thought he was doing what was best for your mom."

"First you were in there threatening him, and now you're defending him? I don't get you."

"I was desperate to get to the truth," Alex said. "I couldn't think of any other way to do it. Now, I think I may have been wrong. Jerrod, that man is your great-grandfather. No matter how mean he is, the fact remains. He's family, and family sticks together. You'd be a better man if you accepted him as he is and showed him more respect. I'm going to have to do the same. I'm afraid I've been as mean as he is. I've been a bad example to you. It escaped all our attention that he dropped everything and ran over here as soon as he heard Jenna had been hurt. I'd say your old granddad has feelings for you guys whether he admits it or not."

"Why did you want me to hear all that stuff?" Jerrod asked. "Mom wouldn't have done that."

"You're in a hard place right now, being a kid, but ready to be a man. This issue has been plaguing you, but your mom hasn't been able to talk about it. Maybe that will change now. But I thought you deserved to hear the truth. Also, I guess I was trying to show your granddad that we're a team now and he can't stand between us anymore."

Jerrod nodded. "Still, I'm pretty mad at him. When he kept you and mom apart, he kept you from us too. You don't understand what that was like for me. Girls aren't so bad, but guys, especially the big mean ones, say some pretty nasty stuff. Some of my friends come from divorced parents, but at least they know who their fathers are. They even get to hang out with them sometimes."

"Are you okay with all this?" Alex asked. "Finding out I'm your dad and all?"

"No need to go into Dr. Phil mode. I'm cool. I even wished it that night when you found me in the lake."

"No kidding? By the way, how is that little bull?"

"I guess that depends on how we cook him." Jerrod grinned.

"Gross."

They stood looking at each other for a moment with their hands in their pockets.

"So, we'll hang out now." Alex smiled. "I'll even show you how to style that haircut to make you look like a rock star."

Jerrod punched him in the shoulder.

****

The next afternoon, Jenna was released from the hospital. Lacey opted to call her grandfather to pick them up. She could use the excuse that Alex was in the middle of his workday and she didn't want to interrupt him. The truth was, she didn't have the courage to face him. Instead, she had to listen to a good old-fashioned Clarence Carlyle lecture.

"What the Sam Hill were you thinking, racing your horse like that? You damn near got yourself killed. A girl should be taught to wear pretty dresses and do girl things." That last comment was undoubtedly meant for Lacey. "In my day, women were proud to be women. They didn't feel the need to act like men."

Lacey and Jenna silently nodded. Now and then they'd throw out a *Yes, Sir*. A car was a confined space, not conducive to arguments. Not until the car had stopped in the Double J drive. That's when Clarence crossed the line. "That poor horse of yours is probably lame now and waiting to be put down."

Jenna burst into sobs and held her head.

"Granddad, I'd shoot you before I'd shoot that horse. I guess you'd better hope she's okay." Lacey didn't invite her grandfather to stay.

She settled Jenna into bed with one of the pills the hospital had provided. After a shower, she changed into clean clothes and went back to check on her. She heard Jerrod's voice as she opened the door.

"It was really cool. Alex made Granddad spill his guts about everything. He said Mom came up pregnant right after Alex took off. Then she got hugely fat and rolled all the way down the stairs at his house. Next thing ya know, we popped out too early and Mom was a mess."

"That's not exactly the way it happened," Lacey said from behind him.

Jerrod jumped off the side of the bed and turned to face her. "Okay, so I paraphrased a little. I don't remember his specific words."

"He said all of this right in front of you?" Lacey asked. "Why would he do that?"

"Alex made him," Jerrod said proudly. "He says we're a team and we stick together. But now he wants us to let Granddad on the team too. That's gonna suck."

"I'm just glad everybody knows." Jenna sighed. "It's hard keeping a secret like that."

Jerrod turned to his mother. "You told her?" the question sounded more like an accusation.

"No, she figured it out on her own," Lacey replied.

"Well, aren't you a friggin' genius." He jumped back to sit on the side on the bed. "So, what's it like to be on drugs?"

"My head hurt like crazy, but I didn't care. I was like, super happy," Jenna answered. "Then bam! I was down for the count."

"Yeah, you probably slept the whole time I was doing your chores. You're going to owe me big time."

"No way," Jenna laughed. "This is payback for the week after you fell through the porch."

Lacey loved the lighthearted banter between her children, but too much excitement would cause Jenna's head to hurt again. She remembered the concussion she'd had when they were born. "That's enough, you two." She pulled Jerrod off the bed and toward the door.

Jenna's cell phone rang. "Oh, it's Alex!"

"Don't talk too long," Lacey warned. "You need your rest."

Lacey had just finished the supper dishes and stepped outside to sit on the porch steps when Ben's truck lights bobbed down the driveway. She first thought it might be Alex. He hadn't answered his phone since he left the hospital, but he'd called both of the kids. She supposed he wasn't ready to talk about what he'd learned at the hospital.

She wasn't looking forward to the conversation either, but now that the cat was out of the bag, so to speak, she was ready to get it over with. She'd hidden the truth long enough.

Ben parked his truck beside the barn. He waved as he went inside to help Darrel finish the evening chores. They'd decided to let Darrel work from sunup to sundown every Tuesday and Thursday, and then straight through the weekend. Ben worked for the auto garage in town during the week, and now, would also spend weekends at the farm. They were both strong and smart, but she suspected that Ben picked up a lot of Darrel's slack.

At first, she didn't know how she'd keep them busy. She insisted Jerrod and Jenna still do their part. But the Taylor boys didn't need a lot of instruction, and before she knew it, repairs were being planned all over the farm. Even the house was likely to get a few improvements soon.

Ben seemed to be the planner. He was extremely detail oriented. It was hard to believe he was only nineteen, but she'd had a lot of responsibilities at that age too.

It was a shame that all their earnings were going into savings for Darrel's college tuition, while Ben worked on cars to make ends meet for them and their grandmother. He was an intelligent boy and, given the chance, he could do better.

Both of them were quickly weaving themselves into the family. Even Buck, her suspicious male herd dog, was warming up to Ben. The boys were getting so familiar with her family; Lacey decided she should have a talk with them.

When she entered the barn, Ben was doling out flakes of hay while Darrel filled water containers. They smiled her way and continued working.

"We wrapped Buttercup's legs to be safe and she looks as right as rain now," Ben said. "How's Jenna feeling?"

"She's doing fine. I appreciate your staying with Jerrod while she was in the hospital. But I wanted to talk to both of you before you leave."

The Taylor boys exchanged wary glances. "Is there a problem, Ms. Carlyle?" Darrel asked. "If we've missed any chores or done anything wrong, we'd we glad to fix it."

"Your work has been fine, better than fine. It's just that the two of you are becoming part of this place, and, well...Indian Lakes is a small town. People tend to entertain themselves with gossip."

A look of misery crossed the boys'faces as they exchanged another glance. Darrel wound the water hose and upended the empty bucket to dry. Ben hung the pitchfork on the wall with the other barn tools.

"I didn't expect word to travel this far," Ben said.

"We're not anything like our parents, Ms. Carlyle," Darrel followed.

"I guess you'll want us to leave," Ben added.

"Leave! No!" Lacey was completely bewildered by the boys' words. "I don't know what you're talking about. I didn't even know you had parents."

Ben took in a deep breath of relief.

"Of course we've got parents." Darrel rolled his eyes. "Everybody has parents."

"I lost mine when I was your age, Darrel," Lacey

informed him. "I lived with my grandfather after they died."

"I'm sorry to hear that, Ms. Carlyle," Ben said. "It's only right, since we're working for you, that we tell you the truth. Our parents are…incarcerated."

Lacey gasped. "I'm so sorry."

"I'm not," Darrel blurted. "They deserve to be where they are."

Ben lightly shoved his brother. "Cut it out, Darrel. Let Ms. Carlyle say what she came here to say."

"Well, I think you just demonstrated what I wanted to talk to you about," Lacey said. "All families have certain things they'd rather keep private."

Darrel looked a little confused, but Ben clarified for his benefit. "What I think you're saying, Ms. Carlyle, is what happens on the Double J, stays on the Double J. You don't want us spreading your business around town."

"I wasn't planning to put it quite that way," Lacey smiled, "but I think you've got the idea."

"We know a thing or two about the gossip mill, Ms. Carlyle," Darrel chuckled. "Our granny calls it the devil's party line."

"If anybody has any questions about what goes on here, ma'am, we'll refer them directly to you," Ben added.

After saying goodnight, Lacey left the barn. She stopped outside the door to turn off the water spigot.

"She didn't even ask about, you know," Darrel said behind the closed door. "Most everybody wants to know why they were put away."

"That's because she's not the nosey sort," Ben replied. "She's a lady."

Lacey grinned all the way back to the house. Ben had a few things to learn about women. Even if they are ladies, they can be curious.

The difference is, knowing how, when, and where to get the information you want.

Chapter Twenty-Six

Alex had been rolling the new reality of his fatherhood around in his head until his brain felt bruised. The last thing he needed to see this morning was Lacey's truck pulling into his parking lot. He wasn't ready to talk to her about this, and he didn't feel bad about that. She'd certainly kept the secret from him long enough. Technically, she still hadn't intended for him to know the truth.

In seconds, Donna greeted her in the front office. There was no door to his workspace, and he didn't want Donna to hear their conversation. He walked to the open archway between the two rooms. "Donna, would you mind going out for those office supplies we need?"

"I already ordered them online, boss," she answered proudly. "They'll be here on Monday."

"Well, perhaps you could pick up the supplies we need for the kitchen."

"I got them this morning on my way here." She still smiled.

"How about picking up my dry cleaning then?"

"Not in my job description." Her smile was fading. "I'm your receptionist, not your mother."

"Donna," Alex growled. "Go out somewhere and take a break, dammit."

She jerked open the bottom drawer to her desk and pulled out her purse. "I'll just go over to the diner and have an iced coffee," she huffed. "And I'm not going to bring you one."

After the front door was firmly closed, Alex walked back to his desk and sat. "Damn, iced coffee would be good," he mumbled.

Lacey approached his desk with determined steps. "I need to talk to you, Alex."

"I hope you're here to talk about business. I'm busy. I don't have time to play games." Alex opened a file on his desk and reached for a pencil.

"I wouldn't think of wasting your precious time." Her cheeks were suddenly hot pink. "As a matter of fact, I would have simply called, but you seem to have misplaced your phone."

Alex glanced at the cell phone lying on the upper right corner of his desk. He didn't owe her any explanations.

"I want to talk to you about the boys."

"What boys? Do you have more children hidden somewhere?"

"Don't be an idiot, Alex. I'm talking about Darrel and Ben Taylor. The boys you hired to work on the farm."

"What about them?"

"That's what I want to know. Did you have them checked out before you hired them? Do you know anything about them?"

"They're helping out on a farm. It's not brain surgery or rocket science. They don't have access to your bank accounts or credit cards." The file in front of Alex was for a resort on Myrtle Beach. It would be nice to be there right now, anywhere but here.

"They do have access to my children," Lacey

replied. "My home life and business are one and the same, you know. Jerrod and Jenna's safety comes before anything else. I don't let just anyone off the street move into their lives."

Alex sat back hard against his chair and glared at Lacey. He could almost smell the can of worms that had just been opened. "Oh, you don't have to tell me," he snarled. "You don't even let their own father into their lives."

"That's not fair." Lacey seemed to shrink back a little, or was that just his wishful thinking?

"It's been weeks. In all that time you could have found a few minutes to say, 'Guess what, Alex, these are your kids.' You're seriously going to tell me what's not fair? What about the fact that I never got to hold my babies, see them take their first steps, hear their first words, tuck them into bed at night, walk the floor when they were sick?"

"You weren't there. I wanted you to be there. I prayed you'd come back. Do you think it was fun, being eighteen-years-old and carrying all that responsibility on my own?"

"You didn't have to do it alone," Alex shouted. "You could have found some way to contact me."

"How, Alex-through your family, your friends, all the people who protected you from getting trapped by the town slut?"

"Don't say that." His voice lowered. "I never thought that about you."

Lacey dropped into a chair at the front of his desk. She looked like she'd been deflated. "Let me ask you something." Her voice was barely above a whisper. "If you had stayed that summer, eighteen-years-old, no job, nothing but a high school diploma, no career in sight, would we still be together? Do you think we would have made it, with two babies to feed and care for? Do you seriously think you'd have been prepared for that kind of stress?"

"I don't know." Alex thought back to that time in his life. "I know you had a hard time. Your grandfather told me what happened. I'm sorry for the pain it caused you. I'm sorry for the damage it left behind. I know it must have been hard. I was going through a hard time too. I spent a year in the hospital. The treatments were horrendous. I had one surgery after another, most of them failed. I wasn't at a party either, but I survived too."

"We were too young." Lacey rose from the chair. "We wouldn't have lasted." She started to walk away, and then stopped at the archway, then turned back to him. "It won't work now, either. Do you want to know why?"

"Why?" If she gave him the needing *more* crap again, he'd blow his top.

"Because, all this time I never knew where you were. I didn't know what had happened to you. But you always knew where I was, and you never came back."

Alex was at a loss for words. It didn't feel like a single breath left his body before he heard her truck's engine fade away in the distance.

****

A week passed with the only communication occurring between Alex and the kids. He called each of them at least once a day. Jenna had recovered and was back to most of her everyday chores.

As she and Jerrod knelt on each side of a row of

tomato plants, they filled baskets with the fruit ready to sell. They liked to work at a similar pace, to keep each other company during the hours the garden required. This morning, neither of them had been very talkative.

Finally, Jenna broke the silence. "It isn't like I thought it would be."

"Why do you always start a conversation in the middle?" Jerrod groused. "I don't know if you're talking about tomatoes, the global economy, or life in general."

"I'm talking about finding our father, you dork." Jenna's gloves were grimy. She pushed her wide brimmed hat back with her forearm. "I thought when he and Mom met again, it would be wildly romantic."

"Geez, Jenna, they're old people. It was bad enough to catch them kissing on the front porch." Jerrod cringed. "People their ages are pretty well played out, I think. They're not interested in romantic stuff. They're just looking for companionship."

"Where'd you get an idea like that?" Jenna asked.

"I saw it on the front cover of that old people magazine that Granddad gets." Jerrod stood and stretched his back. His basket was full. "The article was titled, *How to Find a Companion in your Golden Years*. There was a picture of an old man and woman fishing off a pier."

"Mom does like to fish," Jenna mumbled. "I wonder what else old people do together?"

"They go out to dinner and movies a lot, because they get good discounts." Jerrod took a long step between the plants to help Jenna finish filling her basket. "And, according to the TV commercials, they hold hands when they walk around. Then, when they get home, they sit around drinking coffee and talking about insurance."

"I don't know if Mom and Alex are that old."

"They are," Jerrod assured her. "Have you seen that jar of face cream in the bathroom? Mom's always rubbing on some kind of goop. That's to keep her from getting all wrinkled up. Once she and Alex get back together, she'll probably stop doing it and get all pruny looking, like Granddad."

"Do you think they will?" Jenna stood and stretched now, in preparation for carrying her basket to the end of the row. "Do you think they'll get back together?"

"I don't know. They don't seem to get along very well. Maybe we should come up with a plan to help them out."

"I bet if anything happened to Mom, Alex would come running like a scalded ape."

"Yeah, he sure went nuts when you got hurt." Jerrod thought for a moment. "If something like that did happen, they'd see how much they care about each other."

"So what do you think we should do?" Jenna sighed.

"We need to make a plan." Jerrod took on a devious expression.

Chapter Twenty-Seven

Alex stood at the sink in his boxer shorts. The sky was a purplish shade of gray through his kitchen window. Not a single star could be seen through thick evening clouds. A lightning bolt flashed in the far distance.

He took a bite of his bologna sandwich and thought about Lacey's pot roast, meatloaf, fried chicken, and catfish. He tossed the rest of the sandwich into the garbage bin. It tasted like cardboard compared to the memories he'd collected in Lacey's kitchen.

After her visit the week before, he'd thought about nothing but her. She was probably right about them being too young for a lasting relationship, thirteen years ago. But he couldn't believe she had so little faith in them now.

She didn't understand how hurt he'd been by her rejection. Returning to Indian Lakes had been impossible. The thought that she'd chosen another man had haunted him. He'd gone as far as cutting ties with his childhood friends in order to avoid hearing about her.

Now, look what that had gotten him. He'd never learned that she'd stayed alone. He hadn't heard that she'd had children. He didn't know that she'd struggled daily to build a home and business of her own.

Why had he never come back? Pride? What had

caused it all? Interference and misunderstandings. The same things that had caused her to not receive his letters.

That was all in the past. What kept them apart now? Stubbornness, plain and simple.

There was no doubt that he wanted Lacey in his bed on a full-time basis, but that wasn't the only thing he wanted from her. Just as often, he thought about the kids. He pictured them together as a family. He'd been thinking about that even before he'd known they were his. Now, he was obsessed with the idea. Were the twins the big draw? Was there enough love between Lacey and him to make it work in the long run? Neither of them had spoken the L word to the other. Not in the entire time he'd been back. It was too frightening to be that vulnerable again.

The only person he could talk to, to try to sort this out, was Lacey. But she'd already made up her mind she was finished with him. With all the wealth he'd accumulated, he could give her all she needed. Hell, she wouldn't even tell him what it was that she needed. What was he supposed to do, hire a mind reader?

His cell phone on the kitchen table rang. Alex ducked his head to drink from the water tap, a nasty habit he had when he was alone.

The caller ID showed Jenna's name on the display. He picked it up immediately, anxious to hear a friendly voice.

"Hey sugar, how's it going?"

"Not good, Alex," Jenna voice shook. "I think Mom is hurt."

"Hurt?" An instant chill of alarm ran up his spine. "What's wrong? What happened?"

"I don't know? We found her lying on the floor in the barn. Jerrod is out there with her now. I had to come inside to get my phone from the charger. I don't know what to do. We can't carry her inside."

"Don't move her!" Alex was already pulling on a pair of dirty jeans from the laundry room. There was no time to go upstairs. He had his eye on an old T-shirt and a pair of deck shoes. His keys and wallet were still sitting on his desk. "Has she lost consciousness, is she awake? To hell with it, call 911 and I'll be right there."

Alex had been thinking about trading his sporty BMW for something more practical. At the moment, he was glad to have the extra horsepower. He wished he wasn't so far from the farm, but thankfully, he wasn't still living in Orlando. Lacey needed him, and whether she liked it or not, he would be there for her.

Jenna hadn't mentioned any visible injuries or blood. Had he given her the chance before hanging up? He should have kept her on the phone. No, she needed to call 911. That was the most important thing right now.

He wondered if Lacey had been kicked by a horse. Maybe she'd climbed on something and fallen. Maybe she'd passed out because of a medical problem. Even people their age were known to have heart attacks, strokes, embolisms and such. She could have gotten into a poisonous chemical or been bitten by some weird spider or insect. Damn, he hoped an ambulance was on the way. Why hadn't he gotten her grandfather's phone number?

Alex approached a sharp curve in the road. One long roll of thunder was all the warning he received before he drove into a downpour. He turned his windshield wipers on at full speed. They slapped back and forth at the same rate as his heartbeat. The reflection of his high beam headlights caused the rain to appear as a steel curtain. All he could manage was watching the road below by the lower beams. Soon, even that was hidden by the fog that covered the glass. Alex removed his right hand from the steering wheel to turn on the fan to clear it. In that split second, the wind picked up the lightweight car and shoved it sideways off the road. The windshield cleared in time for him to see that the end of a guardrail for a small bridge was on his left instead of his right side. There was no road in front of him. There was nothing at all.

****

Lacey was tired from giving three riding lessons that afternoon. Still, she made supper and was just finishing cleaning the kitchen. The twins were upstairs, working on their reading list books. The storm as so heavy, she couldn't see the lake.

"Jenna, Jerrod, you'd better get your showers early tonight," Lacey called from the foot of the stairs. "This storm looks like it's going to be a bad one. We may lose power before the night's over."

Jerrod came to the railing wearing a worried expression. "I sure didn't see this coming. Maybe it'll just blow over real quick."

"I don't think so. I've been watching storms around here since long before you were born." Lacey rubbed the goosebumps on her arms. "I'm betting this is going to be an all-nighter. I've got an uneasy feeling about it, too."

Jenna stepped out of her room to join Jerrod on the landing. They did that silent twin talk thing again that drove Lacey a little crazy. Without speaking a word, Jerrod held his hands out to his sides, like he was asking a question. Jenna shrugged. Next, Jerrod pointed at his wrist where an invisible watch might be. Jenna nodded. Jerrod gave her a stern look. She shook her head and scowled. He let out a deep sigh. They both looked as though the weight of the world rested on their shoulders.

"Mom," Jerrod finally said, "we may have done something that's going to make you mad."

Just then, Jenna's cell phone rang. She pulled it from her pocket so frantically it almost fell to the floor. Her face turned even whiter as she fumbled to open it. A second later she flew down the stairs.

"It's Alex," she said. "But all I hear is a weird noise."

Lacey took the phone and held it to her ear. There was a long steady blaring sound on the other end. Then, it was joined by a momentary scraping noise, and then a clap of thunder. Next, a deep gravelly voice whispered, "Need help."

"He must be in his car. I can hear the horn blaring. He needs help!" Lacey swung around to look out the window. "He's out in this storm. I think he's had an accident!" She spoke into the phone in a firm, confident voice. "Alex, we're coming. Just hang on. We'll find you. Close your phone if you can. Try to save the battery."

"We're sorry, Mom," Jerrod began.

"Let me think," Lacey snapped. What could she do? She didn't even know where he was. What would Alex do in her place?

"Jenna, call 911. I have a feeling you know where

he was going."

"Jerrod, you saddle Stardust and Drifter. Alex may be off the road somewhere. And, grab a rope, just in case we need it."

Jerrod jerked a jacket from a hook by the door and was gone.

"I want to go with you," Jenna cried.

"No," Lacey declared. "I can't watch both of you and look for Alex too. I'll call you if there's any news. You call me if you hear anything. If you get scared, call Granddad, but leave the house phone free."

"Shouldn't I call the neighbors to start a search party?" Jenna asked.

"No." Lacey rolled a small blanket into a cylinder shape the size of a bread loaf and slid it into a plastic grocery bag, and then another bag. "I don't want to put anyone else in danger out in this storm." She chose the two largest flashlights from the laundry room shelf, and then two pocket-sized lights. She turned each on to check them. "If we work fast, we may be able to hear his car horn before the battery dies." She stopped to hug her daughter. "We can do this. You just hang tough."

Chapter Twenty-Eight

Neither of the horses appreciated being taken out into the storm. With each clap of thunder, and flash of lightning, they nickered and skipped sideways. It was a chore to keep them moving away from the ranch and deeper into the darkness.

Lacey was confident in the knowledge that she'd taught Jerrod to ride well. The twins could both ride their own mounts before they could tie their shoes. This was the payoff. Getting to Alex fast could mean the difference between life and death. She prayed they weren't already too late.

If Alex had been on his way to the farm as she suspected, he wouldn't have needed to take a side road. She watched the shoulders of the highway for ruts or skid marks, but each side held standing water. The shallow ditches were already full.

Tilting her face straight up into the rain, the sky looked like a sheet of black burlap shedding thousands of silver needles. Not one star twinkled. Not one moonbeam broke through the heavy cloud cover. After thirty years of living in this area, Lacey felt lost. Nothing looked as it should.

Jerrod hadn't said a word since they'd left the farm. His serious, determined expression only reminded her more of Alex. As he searched his side of the road, he matched Stardust's slow gait on Drifter. His shoulders slumped over his loose spine as he swayed in the saddle. The hood of his sweatshirt was pulled up under his hat, shielding his ears.

Drifter did something she'd never seen him do before. In the middle of the Shadow Creek Bridge, he whinnied and stepped backward, refusing to follow Jerrod's commands.

"Something is wrong," she hollered over the cacophony of the storm.

They dismounted near each side of the bridge and directed their flashlights over the railing.

"Over here!" Jerrod shouted.

Lacey ran to join him on the other side.

The water rushed over the nose of the little BMW sports car. It was caught against the side of a large live oak. As the water level rose the car would eventually turn sideways and be swept away. The creek wasn't wide, by normal standards, but wide enough to carry the car between its embankments. It also wasn't deep, but when swollen, could easily fill the inside of the small car. Instinct told her that Alex was trapped inside that car. If he was unconscious, he could drown without ever waking.

They ran to the far end of the bridge. Drifter didn't resist being pulled along: Stardust followed behind.

Lacey grabbed the rope from around Drifter's saddle horn. "I'm going down there."

"No. This is on me, Mom." Jerrod jerked the rope from her hand and quickly began tying it around his waist. "It's my fault that this happened. Besides that, I'm smaller and it would be easier for you to hold my weight."

A lump of lead formed in Lacey's stomach as

Jerrod descended. She'd lost her family once before. She knew she couldn't survive losing Jerrod or Alex.

Holding the rope made using her cell phone impossible. She waited until Jerrod had reached the car and gave him a little extra slack before wrapping it twice around a tree and tying it securely. Then she opened her phone and called 911.

****

Alex hurt all over. The lights and horn of his car had died some time ago. Blacking in and out made time hard to measure. He hoped help would arrive soon, but if it didn't, at least he'd had the chance to hear Lacey's voice one last time.

A loud thump sounded on the roof above his head. A pair of jean clad legs slid down between his window and the tree that held him in place. It was followed by Jerrod's concerned face.

"You look like shit," Jerrod stated. "Your face has blood all over it. Are you badly hurt anywhere else?"

"Everywhere," Alex croaked. "Better than the car though."

"To hell with the car." Jerrod used his flashlight to inspect the rest of Alex's condition. He scowled. "It was time to trade up anyway. Can you move your legs at all?"

"Don't know," Alex said, struggling to stay conscious. "Sorry 'bout this. I'm supposed to be the hero in this family."

"That's okay." Jerrod smiled. "You've saved me twice, so I guess I still owe you one. Besides, getting to be the hero now and then is good for my self-esteem."

"I'll have to remember that…" Alex passed out before the blue and red lights of several rescue vehicles pulsed over the landscape.

****

Hospitals are the coldest places in the world. Being soaked to the skin, it felt like sitting in a meat locker. A nurse had taken pity on Lacey and provided a little white blanket. It wasn't big enough to cover more than her torso. Luckily she didn't carry matches, or she'd have made a bonfire with the spindly coffee table in the waiting room. The same coffee table she'd seen barely more than a week ago. She seriously needed to examine her karma.

The vinyl-covered chairs didn't offer any warmth either, but they had more cushion than the saddle she'd spent most of her day in. It's too bad Lake Regional didn't provide hot baths and dry clothes for their visitors.

After Alex had been loaded into the ambulance, she'd ridden back to the Double J with Jerrod. He'd insisted that he could take both horses home, but it was still stormy and dark. Alex was secure. She couldn't risk Jerrod's health or safety any further.

She didn't even go inside the barn once she'd gotten there. She'd handed Stardust over to Jerrod and went straight to the truck. She said she'd call as soon as she knew something. So far, she didn't know anything. Not a single soul had come through those heavy double doors she'd been staring at.

Behind her in the hallway came the sound of several hurried footsteps and her grandfather's voice.

"You kids slow down before they have to carry me off to the cardiac unit."

He and the twins entered the room, all wearing rain slickers and wide brimmed hats. She recognized her own slicker over Jerrod's left arm and a dry pair of her boots in his right hand. Jenna held a plastic shopping bag.

"Have you heard anything?" Jerrod asked.

Clarence shook his slicker out in the corner and hung it on a rack. "Of course she hasn't. She would have called. It takes a coon's age to find out anything in these damn places."

"I brought you a set of dry clothes and a hairbrush, Mom." Jenna held out the bag. "I knew you'd be as soaked as Jerrod was."

Lacey quickly stood, carrying the bag toward the ladies room. "Sit down and don't take your eyes off those doors. If anyone steps through them, come and get me."

She locked the door and stripped off her sodden clothes, tossing each piece into the sink. The little white blanket made a better towel then it had a blanket. The bone rattling chills were finally dissipating.

The first item she pulled out of the bag was her big, ugly, brown, comfy cardigan. The softness of it nearly brought tears to her eyes. It smelled like home. Next, she found a pair of jeans and a scoop-neck, black T-shirt with the Aerosmith logo on the front. They wouldn't have been her first choice, but they were dry. In the bottom of the bag were the promised hairbrush, which she now saw was badly needed, and a thick pair of socks. Lastly, she pulled out the sexy, pale blue, lace bra and panty set Jenna had bought her on her last birthday. They were supposed to be incentive for her to start dating again. Recalling how red Jerrod's face had turned when she'd pulled them from the little gift bag that day, brought a smile to her face. Again, not what she'd have chosen, but who would know?

Back in the waiting room, the twins laid at each end of a small sofa, their eyes glued to the doors. Her grandfather was in the chair next to the one she'd been using. Two cups of piping hot coffee sat before him.

"I'm sorry you were dragged out at such a late hour, Granddad."

"It's not the first time," he told her, holding out one of the cups. "This is the same hospital John and Lily were brought to after the accident."

"I didn't know." The cup felt warm between her hands. "I was at a sleepover with a friend that night. When the police tracked me down there, they told my friends parents to keep me until someone came for me. I was furious. I'm glad you brought the twins. I know better than anyone how badly they need to be here."

"I didn't handle that situation well, with the accident and all. That was the worst night of my life. I don't like thinking about it." Clarence hung his head.

"But you do. You think about it too much. You've let it turn your heart to stone. That and what happened with my grandmother."

"What do I need with a heart, anyway?" Clarence scoffed.

"They weren't your whole family, Granddad. I needed you." Lacey nodded toward the kids. "They could have been a bigger part of your life, but you were so blinded by self-pity, you couldn't see any of us."

Clarence folded his arms and look straight ahead, pouting like a stubborn child.

"Tonight, when I saw Alex's car in that creek, it was like living it all over again, Mom and Dad's accident I mean."

Clarence didn't bat an eye.

"Do you know I was never invited to a friend's house after that? The other kids felt sorry for me, but they acted like I was cursed. They were afraid something bad would happen if they hung around with me."

"That's ridiculous." Clarence huffed indignantly.

"Alex was my only friend after that day. I'd have gone insane if he hadn't been there for me."

"Are you sure that's not what attracts you to him now?" Clarence looked at her accusingly. "Are you sure you're not just grabbing a hold of the past, trying to recapture your glory days?"

"It's not like that, Granddad," Lacey assured him. "Alex is different now. He's not the same boy who left Indian Lakes thirteen years ago. I've had to get to know him all over again, and I like this Alex an awful lot so far. I may even love him."

"Is that right? Well, when do you suppose you'll know for sure? When you get your hands on the deed to that old farm?"

"It's not like that!" Lacey replied. "I'd give the farm up tomorrow if he wanted me to. I'd never do that for any other man."

"I guess you've made up your mind then."

"I guess I have." Lacey was surprised by the freedom she felt having spoken those words.

A scuffle broke out on the sofa. It seemed the silent twin talk had taken an aggressive turn. Jenna kicked her feet out, causing Jerrod's legs to fall. He sat up and shoved her legs off as well. Using their hands they pushed at each other's shoulders. Both wore a scowl.

"What is wrong with you two?" Lacey snapped in a

loud whisper. "Have you forgotten where you are?"

"It was all his idea," Jenna cried.

"She's the one that made the phone call," Jerrod growled.

"I did what you told me to do." Jenna turned on him.

"That's because you're the most convincing liar I know. You should be on Broadway."

Suddenly Lacey remembered that the twins were about to make a confession before Alex had called. "Exactly what did the two of you do?" Lacey asked, emphasizing the *two*.

"We didn't want you and Alex to break up," Jenna began.

"We wanted you both to see how much you care about each other," Jerrod added.

"Cut the crap and get straight to the mechanics," Lacey demanded.

The twins admitted all.

Tears threatened Lacey's eyes when she realized Alex had risked life and limb for her. She'd sat in his office and cut him down to a nub, and still he rushed to her rescue. She couldn't think about that right now. She had to make sure he was going to be okay first.

"Do the two of you see what your deception has caused? You are not going to get away with it. There will be penance to pay for your lying."

"Aren't we suffering enough?" Jerrod groaned.

Lacey held both of her hands out, palms up. "Hand them over."

Jenna gasped. "No, Mom, please don't do this!"

Lacey's hands remained out. She was in no mood to negotiate. Each kid placed their cell phone in her opened palms with a miserable sigh.

"You can check these out from me when you leave the house, and that won't be often. Even then, they'll only be used for emergencies."

"That's not fair!" Jenna cried.

"Not fair?" Lacey rounded on her daughter. A sob tore from her throat, but she was determined to hold back the tears. "What's not fair is that Alex is in the hospital, because of the lies you told."

"We're so sorry." Jerrod was near tears himself. "I never thought anyone would get hurt."

"Please don't hate us," Jenna added dramatically.

Lacey was determined to stand her ground, but before she could say another word the double doors swung to each side and a doctor walked through with a nurse following closely. "Are you Mrs. Benson?" the doctor asked.

"No," Lacey murmured. They'd finally come with news and now her voice was failing her. "I'm Lacey Carlyle."

"She's his fiancée," Jenna blurted.

Lacey pinned her daughter with a stern look, but Jenna just shrugged.

"Oh, good," the doctor said with a show of relief. "My name is Doctor Dean Bennett. I've been with Alex since he came in. I'm sorry it's taken me so long to speak to you. We had to clean him up and check out so many little injuries. Luckily, they were mostly from small shards of glass and twigs. He did have a large gash over his forehead that required quite a few stitches. The blow he suffered in that area is the reason he lost consciousness. We'll have to keep an eye on that for at least twenty-four hours. His left arm was broken in two places and we had to take him in for surgery. He'll have some hardware to deal with for a while. Lastly, his leg was twisted in the wreckage. Everything seems all right now, but it's going to hurt like the dickens. He'll wear a soft cast on it for a few weeks."

The nurse held a small bag out to Lacey. "We'll be moving Mr. Benson to a private room while he's unconscious. It would be best for you to take his personal items with you. He had a cell phone, keys and a wallet in his pockets. His clothes and shoes aren't salvageable." The nurse was matter-of-fact in her speech, but her eyes showed compassion. "Is there anyone we can call for you, Ms. Carlyle?"

"Oh, yes." Lacey fumbled inside the bag for Alex's cell phone. "Could you please inform his parents? I'm sure they'll have a lot of questions and, well, they'd much rather talk to you."

The nurse raised a brow. She knew exactly what Lacey was not saying. "Certainly, ma'am," she said gently, as she jotted down the number from Alex's phone.

Before he retreated back through the double doors, the doctor stopped. "It doesn't make a difference in his treatment, but could I ask—" He hesitated uncomfortably—"how he received such a massive amount of scars?"

"He was near an explosion aboard ship when he was in the Navy, thirteen years ago come December." Lacey sighed. "We were both in the hospital that Christmas, half a world away from each other."

"Good Lord," Clarence mumbled. "I didn't know."

"Neither did I, Granddad. We've both suffered and we both have a lot to make up for."

Chapter Twenty-Nine

Alex felt cold, his mouth was dry, and his head was pounding. When he tried to reach the blanket that had slid down to his waist, his left arm wouldn't budge. It ached and felt like it weighted fifty pounds. After forcing one eyelid open, he saw that his arm was encased in metal and plaster. Both eyes popped open wide to check that out. He reached his right hand over to touch it and noticed the IV line in that arm.

A rustling noise at the side of the strange, narrow bed caught his attention. He looked over the two-foot length of metal railing. A nurse knelt beside him.

"Is this thing capable of picking up a good country station?" Alex pointed at the contraption on his left arm.

The nurse laughed. "Good Morning, Mr. Benson. That's not usually the first thing a person asks when they wake up." The nametag on her scrub top read: Linda.

"Okay then, let's try this one, Linda." His brow lifted sending a sharp pain to the sore spot on his head. "Are you doing what I think you are down there?"

"I'm emptying your catheter bag. You had surgery on your arm. You've had anesthesia and been unconscious for some time now."

"Do I have any injuries south of my belly button?"

"One leg was sprained and badly bruised." She

took the half full container to the adjoining restroom and washed her hands.

"I don't know if I'm buying that as a good reason to tube my little buddy."

Linda smiled and held a straw to his lips. Alex sucked in a mouthful of ice water and held it for a moment before swallowing.

"I'll talk to the charge nurse and see if we can switch you to a portable urinal," she said.

"I'll have to get up soon anyway," Alex shifted in the bed trying to get comfortable. Where were the controls for the stupid thing? "A nice hot shower is the only thing that'll make me feel human again."

"No showers for you, not until we can remove some of that apparatus from your arm. I'll call an orderly who can take you down to the therapy department. A nice whirlpool bath would be good for that leg."

"Oh hell no," Alex grabbed the right side rail and lifted himself into a sitting position. The pain in his head exploded and the room swayed. His right leg felt like it had been caught in a vise and twisted a few turns. "You're not taking me to the dungeon to stick me in a torture vat. Been there, done that, and next time, someone is going to die a slow painful death."

"Settle down, Mr. Benson." Linda raised the head of the bed, hoping he'd relax against it. He did. He had no other choice. "I'll see if someone's free to give you a sponge bath."

"I don't need some big, ugly guy coming in here to handle my junk. Just bring me the stuff and I'll do it myself." Alex was so upset by memories of his last hospital stay he didn't realize that Lacey had been listening from the doorway.

"Take it easy, big guy." Lacey sauntered toward him looking like an angel in an Aerosmith T-shirt. "I won't let that little nurse hurt you."

"Lacey!" Alex tried once again to sit up on his own, but immediately fell back with a grimace. "Are you okay? What happened to you? Jenna said you'd been hurt!"

"Jenna lied. Jerrod was in on it too. They were trying to get us back together. I'm sorry, Alex."

Alex gave a soft chuckle. It was all he could manage with his pain. "I'm not sorry. Their hearts were in the right places. I'm just glad you're okay. I was so afraid something awful had happened to you. I couldn't stand to lose you again. I wouldn't survive it a second time."

"The kids are still going to be punished, Alex." Lacey put on her bossy face. "They nearly got you killed. I don't want to lose you either."

Lacey's small hand fit perfectly inside his large one.

The conversation was obviously turning personal. The nurse gathered her things and left the room.

"I'll leave that up to you, babe. You're the expert in that field." Suddenly Alex had another thought. "Damn! What am I going to do about the office? Donna isn't ready to handle the place on her own. She hasn't even figured out the coffeemaker."

"Calm down." Lacey leaned over to smooth his messy hair. "I called Mary Ann. She's sending someone down from the closest office in Georgia."

Then something new stole Alex's attention. He hooked a finger into the scooped neck of Lacey's shirt and took a peek. "What are you wearing under there? Is that blue lace?"

"Alex!" Lacey tried to jump out of his reach, but he'd grabbed the hem of her shirt. The tug caused the neckline to pull lower, exposing the lace trim.

"It is," Alex teased. "My country girl is hiding city girl frillies." In a flash, he released her shirt and grabbed the waistband of her jeans. "What kind of panties do you have on?"

Even though he was injured, Lacey couldn't pull his hand away with both of hers. She squealed with laughter when he used his index finger to tickle her belly button.

"If I wasn't in such a mess, I'd let you have your wicked way with me, woman." Alex chuckled.

"I once heard a wise man say, there's more than one way to skin a cat," Lacey replied.

"Hmm, despite my aversion to skinning cats, I admire the man's thinking."

"Perhaps." She kissed his lips. "But I suspect that's the drugs talking."

"What is going on in here?" a woman shouted from the doorway.

Alex and Lacey's heads snapped in her direction. They felt like a couple of teenagers, caught necking under the school bleachers.

Alex had the added torment of an ice pick sharp pain to his head. "Mom!"

Cheryl Benson slowly came around the bed where Lacey stood frozen. Her lips were held in a straight, severe line. Her narrowed eyes never left Lacey's face. "I should have known you'd have something to do with this. Any time you're near him, my son meets disaster."

Lacey couldn't speak. She couldn't even move back from the angry woman.

"What do you mean by that?" Alex asked.

"How can you even ask?" His mother turned to him with the same irate expression. "Everything changed after you started seeing *her*. You gave up a good scholarship, ran off to the Navy, and then got caught in that horrible explosion. Now, you've moved your company headquarters to this horrid little town, just so you can sleep with *her*. And look where it's gotten you. How can you give up everything you've worked for, for a small town trollop?"

"Let me start by saying, that's all utter bull-shit, Mother," Alex said with a cold glare. "I'll follow that up by telling you, if you call Lacey a name like that again, I'll have you thrown out of this room. I make my own decisions."

"Well!" Cheryl huffed. "We all know reason is beyond you where she's concerned. She tried to make a fool of you. If it hadn't been for me, you'd be trapped in a marriage with a woman of little morals, just to give her child a name. God only knows who the real father might be."

"Not just God," he replied. "I know who left her pregnant. I did an excellent job of making a fool of myself. What I'd like you to tell me is why you didn't say anything to me, all those years ago?"

"I knew how infatuated you were with her." Cheryl looked at Lacey and gave a delicate snort. "I didn't want your heart to be broken when you found out she was trying to trick you."

"But I wasn't," Lacey whispered.

"Why are you even here?" Cheryl yelled. "You

don't belong here. Go back to your dirty little farm and leave my son alone."

A scuffle broke out outside the door. A moment later, David Benson entered with each of the twins in a tight grip. "I found these two hoodlums eavesdropping in the hallway. Can anyone here identify these perpetrators?"

"I'll take custody, Dad," Alex quipped. "Let them go so they can come give their old man a hug."

As the twins raced toward his bed, David stood dumbfounded. "I'll...be...damned," he muttered.

"Somebody will be more than damned if they keep giving my mom a hard time." Jerrod glared at the strange woman beside the bed.

"Slow down little man," Alex chuckled. "I know you're just defending your mom, but then I'd have to defend my mom. And that would be a hard thing to do right now. Besides that, I'm sorry to say, she's your grandmother."

Jenna crawled onto the bed to cuddle under Alex's right arm. "I think all these mean people should go away and leave us alone."

"Well!" Cheryl huffed. "I can see these children weren't taught respect for their elders."

"Hold it right there, girl," Clarence blustered from the doorway. "These kids are the best in town. Lacey's done an excellent job raising them with no help from anyone-and that's our fault. It's about time they brought their family together."

Nurse Linda rushed in next, flustered and pink cheeked. "We can't have this many visitors in one room. Some of you will have to go to the waiting room. The shouting is making the other patients nervous."

David Benson took his wife by the hand. "Come on Cheryl. I need a cup of coffee, and maybe a valium."

"Better make that an order for two," Jerrod sneered. "The old lady needs to settle down."

Alex nudged him.

"Come with me, Lacey," Clarence said. "These kids have been driving me up a wall. Let *him* handle them for a few minutes. That should prove what the man's made of."

The door latch clicked, closing the twins in with their father.

"I'm so sorry." Jenna began to cry.

Jerrod shuffled his feet by the bed. "We really screwed things up, didn't we?"

"Yeah," Alex answered. "You know, your mom was right. I do love you. I always will, no matter what. I'm proud to have two kids as great as you. However, if you ever lie and try to manipulate me or your mother again, I'll kick your butts up between your shoulders."

Chapter Thirty

Alex was released from the hospital the next day. Since the downstairs area of his house was used as office space for East Coast L.D., Lacey decided he should move in with her until he could get around better. It was impossible for him to climb stairs with one crutch and a broken arm. She made space in her living room for a rollaway bed.

For the first week, he felt helpless and confined, but he used the time to learn more about his children. They'd all had long talks and perused old photo albums for hours. He'd been spoiled with good home cooking and constant attention. Still, he pushed himself through an exercise routine every day.

Lacey suspected his exercise had as much to do with sexual frustration as it did regaining his strength. Their new relationship was woefully limited.

Being a resourceful woman, Lacey waited until the church bus left that Sunday. Then, she gave Alex a close and personal lesson on riding western style.

By the second week, he'd traded his crutch for a cane and the cast on his arm was just a normal cast. He'd started working at the office again and was finally able to hobble up the stairs at night.

They only had one more problem to overcome. He still couldn't drive and Lacey's truck was hard for him to get in and out of. Donna began picking him up at

8:00 a.m. and bringing him home at 5:30 every day.

On Friday afternoon of the second week, Lacey was surprised by a visit from Cheryl Benson.

"May I come inside?" the older woman asked.

Lacey wished she could say no, but she was Alex's mother and her own mother's best friend. She'd known her all her life.

"Alex is at work." Lacey held the screen door open and stepped aside.

"Do you think that's wise?" Cheryl asked as she passed. "No. Forget I said that. Alex will do as he pleases." She made a quick scan of the living room, and then added, "You have a charming home."

"No, I don't. Everything is old and worn out, but it's ours. We've worked hard for it and we love it. Would you like to come into the kitchen? I have a pitcher of cold tea in the fridge and I'm in the middle of making supper."

Cheryl sat at the table while Lacey poured them each a cup of coffee. "Whatever you're making smells wonderful. I'm not much of a cook. Never was."

"What brings you back to Indian Lakes, Ms. Benson?" Lacey asked. "We weren't expecting you again so soon."

"I want to see my grandchildren."

"They're working right now. I imagine they'll be in within the hour."

"They work?" Cheryl appeared shocked. "What kind of work could such small children do? They're so young."

"Ms. Benson, this is a working farm. It's the way we make our living. The twins grew up working the fields and tending the livestock. We've never had

228

anyone to count on but each other." Lacey returned to the stove to stir a pot of greens and check the cornbread in the oven. "It would be my guess that Jenna is collecting honey from the bees about now, and Jerrod is grooming the horses that I used today in my riding lessons."

"Jenna and Jerrod, those are nice names. I wish I'd asked what they were when we met them in the hospital." Cheryl stared down into her cup. "I want to get to know them. I'd like them to come to Miami for a visit, before school starts."

"Ms. Benson, I'm not sure that's a good idea right now."

"Alex can fly then down and back in a weekend. If it's a matter of getting the work done here, I'm sure he can hire someone."

"That's not the problem. The kids aren't slaves, they work here because this farm belongs to them as much as me. They care about it. I'm just not sure how they'd feel about going to visit you so soon. We're very protective of each other. You said things about me I wish they hadn't heard."

"I feel terrible about that." Cheryl reached into her purse for a tissue to dab her eyes. "I regret the things I said."

"Help me understand." Lacey sat across the table from her. "You were my mother's best friend. You shared secrets and laughed like young girls together. You attended all my birthday parties. After Mom died, you treated me like trash. What did I do?"

Cheryl sniffed and wiped at her nose. "Your mother was the only friend I had. I came from a poor family. I wanted to be popular in school, but the *hip* kids wouldn't accept me. Your mother's family was poor too, but she didn't seem to mind. She was my opposite. I was bitter and she was sweet. I made a fool of myself one day, trying to get a boy's attention. Everyone laughed except Lily. She taught me that one genuine friend was worth far more than a hundred cheerleaders and football players. I truly loved her.

Still, I didn't want my children to grow up poor. I married well and planned for my sons to have a good future. Travis was already in college when Lily died. I was grieving for her when you and Alex started seeing each other. I felt like you were taking him away from me. I couldn't stand another loss. I wanted to get away from this town as fast as possible and take him with me. When Alex gave up his scholarship, I thought his future was over. I thought he'd end up being a poor laborer like my father. I blamed you."

Then you showed up pregnant, I didn't think the baby could possibly be Alex's. You seemed too far along. I didn't know you were having twins. But I knew Alex loved you enough to stand by you. I knew he'd give up everything for you. I was determined not to let that happen. I slipped right back into being that bitter little schoolgirl. After Alex got hurt, it strengthened my determination to protect him." Cheryl took a deep breath before she added, "I thought I'd finally gotten over all that, until Alex told me he'd moved back here and your name came up. I guess I wasn't as good a friend to your mother as she was to me. She would have done better by a child of mine. I've thought about that a lot over the last two weeks."

The screen door slammed. When they turned, they found the twins holding each handle of a large basket filled with jars of honey. Jenna reached into the basket and removed one of the jars. She held it out.

"Would you like to buy a jar of honey, Ms. Benson?"

Lacey was apprehensive about her children's behavior. Their first meeting with Ms. Benson had been a disaster, but Alex had interceded. She wished Alex was here now.

Jenna's expression was open and pleading. Not for a sale of a jar of honey, but for acceptance. Jerrod, on the other hand looked surly.

"I'd love to buy a jar," Ms. Benson said. "You know, your Uncle Travis's little girls call me Nana."

"Nana," Jerrod sneered. "Look lady, we can call you Grandma, but Nana is out of the question. If you don't like it, we're right back to Ms. Benson. Your choice."

"Grandma it is then," Cheryl smiled. "How much do I owe you for the honey?"

"Oh, I don't know..." Jenna looked at Lacey.

"Five bucks even," Jerrod piped in.

"That sounds fair to me." Cheryl pulled her wallet from her purse and produced a ten-dollar bill. "Do you have change?"

"Nope," Jerrod said. "I guess you'll have to take two jars." He snatched the bill from Cheryl's fingers and reached for a second jar of honey.

"Jerrod!" Lacey exclaimed.

"That's the way I do business on the road, Mom."

"And good business it is," Cheryl agreed. "If the buyer doesn't like it, they can go to town and pay more for the processed kind. These jars even have a piece of the comb inside. You don't get that at a grocery store."

"I could make you a good deal on some strawberry preserves," Jerrod offered.

"Those are Granddad's strawberries," Jenna cried.

"He'll live. A man his age shouldn't eat so many sweets anyway."

"I'm afraid I don't have enough room in my suitcase, and I have to fly home tomorrow." Cheryl laughed. "But you do drive a hard bargain, Jerrod Benson."

"My name is Carlyle, ma'am." Jerrod was suddenly serious. "Jerrod Alexander Carlyle."

Cheryl looked stricken. Lacey could see she didn't know how to respond.

"You kids go upstairs and wash for supper," Lacey said. "When you get back you can set the table for five. I hope your grandmother will stay and eat with us."

"Make that six," Alex said from the doorway. "I ran into your grandfather in town this afternoon and asked him to bring me home. I'd like him to stay for supper as well. That way I can talk to all of you at one time. There are some changes I'm thinking of making."

"I don't want to stay for supper," Clarence declared. "I thawed out a ham steak for my supper tonight."

"It'll keep until tomorrow," Alex said.

"Tomorrow is pan fried steak night."

"For God's sake, Clarence, put some variety in your life."

Alex prodded the old man back through the living room and onto the porch. "I'm offering you a free meal made by the best cook in town, you old buzzard. Be gracious enough to accept." He looked over his shoulder to make sure they were alone. "I don't want to face the dragon alone. I figure, with her on one side of me and Jerrod on the other, I wouldn't stand a chance with a broken arm."

"Ha!" Clarence chuckled. "Maybe I will stay for the show."

"So, why do you think your mother's here? She didn't come up from Miami just to buy honey."

Alex had been so concerned about his mother and Lacey being in the same room, he hadn't stopped to wonder why she had come. He hadn't noticed any screaming or bloodshed. That was a good sign.

Conversation around the supper table was led by the twins, as usual. They loved to talk about the farm. To Alex's relief, his mother asked a few good questions and was properly impressed. The only times he had to send Jerrod a kick under the table was when he'd get too detailed about some aspects of tending livestock. There are things city people are better off not knowing and would definitely rather not hear while they eat.

He had no assistance in monitoring the conversation. Lacey seemed to be in a state between shock and raw nerves. Clarence simply chuckled at Jerrod's inappropriate monologue. Thank God for Jenna and her curiosity about Miami and the Benson family.

When everyone had about finished their dessert, Alex cleared his throat to get their attention. "I'm glad you're all here. I wanted to talk to you about some changes I'm planning to make."

"If you're thinking of putting alpacas on the farm," Jerrod said, "let me stop you now. I hate those things...nasty."

Alex lifted a brow. "No alpacas, I hear you.

However, that's not what I was thinking about. I ordered a new car today. I feel that I'm capable of driving myself now."

"What did you get?" Jerrod nearly jumped from his chair with the enthusiasm that all boys share regarding cars.

Alex raised his hand. "We'll talk about that later. There are other, more important things to discuss right now. I wanted to tell you that I've decided to move away from the office. Donna and her son are going to take over the apartment. It would be more convenient and save them a lot of money. Some help getting them settled would be a nice gesture. They could use more friends."

Lacey looked up at him with her chin tilted up, but her eyes were glassy. Clarence cleared his throat loudly. The twins' faces were frozen in an expression of disappointment and sorrow. Cheryl smoothed the napkin on her lap to avoid everyone's gaze.

"Where are you planning to move to, son?" she asked in a quiet tone.

"That depends." Alex stood and walked around the table to Lacey. "Can I speak to you alone for a moment?"

After guiding Lacey to a chair in the living room, Alex knelt before her on one knee. He'd been practicing and preparing for this since leaving the hospital. "Lacey. I want to stay here on the farm."

When she started to shake her head, Alex added, "Just hear me out, before you say no. I know we've both had a hard time and trust isn't easy for either of us. If you think about it, though, we never intended to hurt each other. I want to put all that behind us. I want us to

234

both forgive the people who pulled us apart, for the kids' sake. They need more than us. They deserve a whole family. I think my mom and your granddad have learned their lesson. If they haven't, they'll find the four of us a force to be reckoned with. But that only works if we stick together."

"I don't know…" Lacey chewed her lower lip.

"Then let me tell you what I know. I know that you're the most precious person in my life. I know you'd be a strong and loyal partner. I know you're the mother of two kids who mean the world to me. And, I know I can't live without you."

"But Alex"

"I'm not finished. Lacey, you drive me crazy, you make me happy, and you accept me as I am. You chase my nightmares away and make me feel whole."

"Oh, Alex…"

"Wait a minute. Lacey, I love you heart and soul. I'm begging you, please, marry me."

Lacey let out a sob as she threw her arms around his neck and hugged him.

"Is this a yes?" he asked. "Have I convinced you?"

"Yes," she said. "You've said enough. You found my *more*. I love you too."

Hoots, whistles, and clapping came from the doorway where the others had been listening. Alex turned on them, frustrated. "I'm not finished yet!"

He dug into his pants pocket for a small velvet covered box. He opened it to reveal a three-carat blue diamond ring. "Would I be throwing my money around if I offered this to you?"

The family rushed in, no longer able to contain themselves.

"I'm glad you're all here," Alex told them. "I may need help getting up."

****

Lacey watched from the window as Alex walked around the front lawn to stretch his leg, her grandfather beside him. They appeared to be in a serious discussion, man to man. It warmed her heart to see Alex place his hand on the other man's shoulder and smile. Buck flanked his other side with tail wagging. She looked down at the ridiculously gorgeous ring on her finger. This day had turned out nearly perfect.

When she turned, she found Cheryl Benson watching her from the door. Lacey took a deep breath.

"I know I'm not what you had in mind for your son," she stated.

"My son has exactly what I wanted for him," Cheryl contradicted. "He has a home, a family, love, happiness. What more could a mother ask for."

"Thank you," Lacey said.

Now the day was perfect.

Epilogue

Lacey waved to her grandfather seated in a lawn chair in front of Westin's Barber Shop. He'd become a regular guest at their table every Friday evening. The twins were fascinated by his boyhood stories and he seemed to enjoy telling them. She didn't think the old man grieved as much anymore.

In a few more weeks, her grandfather would be walking her down the aisle of the church. She and Alex hadn't missed a Sunday service since becoming engaged. The talk around town had turned to speculation about the wedding, instead of the fact that it had been a long time in the making. The other women gave her smiles now instead of sideways glances.

The twins were both looking forward to spending their Christmas break in Miami with the Bensons. Alex had adamantly shot down their suggestion of going along on the honeymoon. Jenna couldn't wait to be a mentor to her two little cousins. Jerrod was looking forward to a deep-sea fishing trip with his Grandpa Benson and Uncle Travis. How spoiled would they be, by the end of two weeks?

Alex looked regal astride Mercury as they trotted alongside her and Stardust. The kids were riding closer to the curb, throwing candy to the children. The Double J Farm marked the end of the Heritage Day Parade.

"Daddy," Jenna said as she rode closer, "can I

spend the night at Vicky's house? She has the whole Twilight collection on DVD. We're going to watch them all back to back."

"Aren't you tired of those movies by now? Well, I guess its okay, as long as I don't have to sit through them again."

"Hey, Dad," Jerrod grinned. "Did you see the way Alison Palmer was waving at me? She likes me, I can tell."

"Way to go, Son," Alex said in mid high-five.

Yes, her life had become so much richer.

A word about the author...

Sandra Dailey is an avid reader and lifelong storyteller. She caught the writing bug after winning a short story contest and has never looked back.

Sandra lives in North Florida with her husband.

You can contact her at:

sandradailey.author@gmail.com
www.sandradailey.com
www.sandradailey.blogspot.com